KU-033-116

'Unwanted child . . . Dad a crook . . .
hopeless at school . . . sisters hate me . . .
Mum picks on me . . .'

munity social worker Bob Laken and
Bet it was another cry for help. Their
at they should move into the
rhood, not just offer help from
meant open door to a non-stop stream

ok tells the story of what happened –
f real people caught in real-life
In turn funny, touching, surprising,
the book is full of humour, grit,
nation and a faith that works in a
here there are no soft options, but
here can be real hope.

aken' is a pseudonym. The author is
Leader of a community project
red by a voluntary society. He has
ously worked with a local authority as a
ial Worker and is the author of several
ooks. Married with two children, he lists as
his 'pet like' being with the family. Playing
football and cricket are close runners-up.
What he most dislikes is Do-it-yourself.

More than a Friend

BOB LAKEN

A LION PAPERBACK
Tring · Belleville · Sydney

Published by
Lion Publishing plc
Icknield Way, Tring, Herts, England
ISBN 0 85648 581 0
Lion Publishing Corporation
10885 Textile Road, Belleville, Michigan 48111, USA
ISBN 0 85648 581 0
Albatross Books
PO Box 320, Sutherland, NSW 2232, Australia
ISBN 0 86760 453 0

First Edition 1984

British Library Cataloguing in Publication Data

Laken, Bob
   More than a friend
   I. Title
   823'.914[F]   PR6062.A/
   ISBN 0-85648-581-0

Phototypeset by Input Typesetting Ltd, London
Printed and bound in Great Britain
by Collins, Glasgow

Contents

Author's Note

The incidents in this story have sometimes
been enlarged or their effects exaggerated.
Certain features of clients' characters and
circumstances have been changed.
Sometimes the time sequence has been re-
arranged. Occasionally an experience of one
person has been transplanted into the life of
another. The book is based on two jobs which
I have undertaken but here I telescope them
into one. All this has been done in order to
hide the real identities of the persons
concerned. Because of these changes I regard
the book as fiction, as a novel. Yet nearly all
the events actually happened, the characters
are based on real people, the experiences are
drawn from my interaction with them.
Perhaps the book can best be described as true
fiction.

1
Moving In

I was struggling to edge the settee through the narrow door of our council house. My wife, Bet, was slowly sinking under its weight. A hand tapped on my shoulder. With my nose buried deep in the settee, I heard the voice.

'Got a spare room?'

We lowered the ponderous piece of furniture, jamming it between the doorposts, and turned round. The speaker was a filthy old man, with uncut hair, unshaven chin and unwiped nose. His voice was a whine.

'Heard you were moving in. You've got no kids, so you could do with some company – and I could help with the cooking.'

Looking at his grimy hands, I could think of nobody I'd less like to touch our food. Nonetheless, after shoving the settee through, we invited him in.

The elderly gent introduced himself as Lionel and with the help of four cups of tea and two packets of biscuits he told his pitiful story. He had once, so he said, been a successful businessman, commercial traveller, newspaper reporter and professional tennis coach. Unfortunately, due to events beyond his control, he was now penniless and living off social security. He dwelt on the cruelties of his landlord who, if Lionel were to be believed, locked him out if he came in after 9 p.m., stole from his room, charged exorbitant rents and was insanely jealous of him.

Thankfully, I was able to point out that our tenancy with the council expressly forbade the taking in of lodgers. Lionel stayed another hour, moved on to the sandwiches, and only left when I asked if he would help bring in the rest of the furniture from the removal van.

After Lionel had taken himself off, Bet sank into the sofa and laughed.

'Well, you wanted a job that brought you close to local people. Looked to me as though you were keeping your distance.'

I grinned back. Bet is a slim, black-haired, olive-skinned cockney. As I looked at her laughing face, I wondered again if her dark features went back to Jewish or Southern European stock. We'd been brought up in the same part of East London. Her father had been the projectionist at the local cinema. My dad had run a removal van. After leaving school, I worked with him, helping out at a youth club in the evenings. Encouraged by the club's leader, I eventually went to college to train as a social worker. While there I again met Bet – who was pursuing a teaching certificate – not having seen her since the days we were regulars at the Saturday morning pictures. We married soon after leaving college and both obtained jobs with the same council. Bet taught at an infants school and I was a social worker with the Social Services Department.

That Social Services Department was located in a huge tower block. For four years I shared a room, known as 'the factory', with twenty-five other social workers. Each weekday we would pack our notebooks and forms into our briefcases, sally forth from the headquarters and drive out to the city's inner ring, or the sprawling estates to see our clients.

After the first confusing year, during which clients grumbled that I was 'too hard' while my superiors warned me about being 'too soft', I settled down. I even devised a routine for dividing my time between the elderly, the physically handicapped, the mentally ill, delinquents and children in the care of the local authority. But I never felt wholly satisfied, sensing that I had somehow turned into an official who was too far removed from the very people I wanted to help.

Bet opened my eyes when she pointed out that I had been closer to people when lugging furniture around for my dad and mixing with teenagers in the evening. Since I was a Christian, I wanted to apply Christian principles to my life.

It's obvious to anyone who reads the gospels that Jesus, the carpenter's son, had not separated himself from people in need. Far from it. He walked beside them, shared meals, regarded them as friends. He lived amongst them and was one of them. That was what I wanted to do. Then I saw an advert for a 'community social worker'. We sent for details which informed us that the Edgely Branch of the Community Christian Council wanted to appoint a worker, initially for three years. He would live in a council house on a local authority estate and use his time and talents to stop families from needlessly splitting up, prevent delinquency and help youngsters in the area. Bet urged me to apply, even though a move would entail her leaving a teaching post where she was happy. The salary for the advertised post was small, the future after three years was uncertain, but the idea of working within a small neighbourhood appealed to both of us.

I applied, obtained the position, and early that same Autumn I drove dad's lorry from London and we carted our furniture into a small two-bedroomed council house.

The day after moving in, Bet and I drove round Edgely in our mini-van. Edgely was a forty-year-old council estate situated five miles from the centre of a West Country town. It did not suffer the raw appearance of some modern estates and new towns. Time had mellowed the grey stone and a few trees had grown to maturity. The houses were small but I'd been informed that successive modernization schemes had ensured that all possessed bathrooms and indoor toilets.

Apart from houses, there seemed little else. We spotted a pub, a small working-men's club, a couple of churches and a shop. In the distance we could see extensive farmland, yet within the estate kids had little if any space where they could play in safety. We saw some kicking a ball around in the street and others gathered outside some lock-up garages whose walls were decorated with graffiti – some humorous, some obscene.

The estate was bounded on the west and south by two busy trunk roads. To the east and north the council houses changed into a mixture of small, new, private semis and Victorian, artisan-type terraced buildings. Despite being a planned local authority scheme, the roads did not suffer from excessive straightness. They curved, came to a dead end, were interrupted by small groves and cul-de-sacs. Most houses had gardens. Some were neatly kept with flower beds and small lawns guarded by an army of gnomes. To enter others was like going on safari through knee-high grass, flattened gates and broken-down fences.

We stopped outside the shop. It was open, although we were calling on a Sunday morning. No wares were displayed in the two windows. Instead, the back view of brown peg-board presented a drab, off-putting appearance. We stepped inside. The shop served as a post office, off-licence, butcher's, grocer's, green grocer's and general store. Goods were piled everywhere. A few shoppers were chatting with two female shop assistants. They looked us up and down, obviously knowing that we were strangers.

'You must be Bob Laken. The vicar said you were coming.'

The speaker was the shop owner. Red Moore was a copper-haired, stocky, middle-aged man who (we learnt later) had lived over the shop for twenty years. He shook hands with both of us and summoned his wife, Dixie, two teenage daughters, an Alsatian and a red setter to meet us.

'You've not taken on an easy job. I expect you know about the estate's reputation.'

I nodded. He was referring to incidents of delinquency and vandalism which were sometimes splashed across the local paper.

'Still, you could do a good job,' Red continued. 'The kids need something to occupy them, someone to take an interest in them. The council's done nothing here. Just put up houses as far away from the town centre as possible and then left people alone. Let me know if I can help – and feel free to stick up any notices.'

He pointed to a board on which were stuck scraps of paper advertising church services, a cot for sale and women looking for domestic work. Bet and I left, feeling cheered that at least one family was welcoming our arrival.

The same afternoon we had an appointment with the local vicar. Parking outside the parish church, we reckoned it was built in the 1950s. The church seemed all roof, like an enormous triangle stuck on a border of glass. Next door was a lower, older, brick building bearing the title 'St Matthew's Church Hall'. Adjoining the hall stood a modern vicarage, the home of the Rev. Charles Wantage. I had met Charlie at the job interview. He must have spotted our arrival, for he had opened the door even before we knocked. He gave us both a bear-like hug.

'Welcome – and come in. The family's out, I'm afraid. My wife's taken them to play cricket. Play cricket do you? Good – I must put you in the St Matthew's team.'

Charlie ushered us into the kitchen. Papers and books were scattered everywhere. He attempted to make coffee. Bet came to his rescue, finding the coffee under some black robes and the milk on the doorstep. The sugar bowl was retrieved from a circle of puppies on the floor.

Once we were seated on some kitchen stools, Charlie talked to us about Edgely. Like many vicars, he was overworked and underpaid, but the strain had not dimmed his energy or enthusiasm. He emerged as a man of great compassion, dedicated to serving God and people. St Matthew's attracted a large congregation but to his regret very few were drawn from the council estate. Most travelled in from private houses in the nearby suburbs, no doubt drawn by Charlie's lively personality and powerful preaching. A church youth club held only the offspring of church members and failed to draw in the estate children. Feeling that his church was irrelevant to the lives of many local families and saddened by Edgely's vandalism and delinquency, Charlie had turned to the Community Christian Council. Up till then the Council had devoted its meagre funds to the deprived inner ring areas of large cities. Charlie persuaded its committee to fund a worker for Edgely. Then he talked the local Housing Department into providing a council house for the worker. He told us as

11

much as he could about the estate. And he offered the occasional use of the church hall – although it was heavily booked by the Whist Drive, the St Matthew's Players, The Evergreen Vegetarian Society, the Darby and Joan Club, and the Professional Women's Circle.

'Apart from that, you're on your own,' he grinned. 'No, not on your own, there's always help from upstairs.'

Bet and I glanced upwards, not sure whether Charlie had some secret weapon in his bedroom, or was indicating that our faith should be in God. More enthusiastic hugs and we returned to the mini.

Monday morning, early September. Bet was already up. She had obtained a post at the local infant school and was about to start her first day. She came into the bedroom to kiss me goodbye.

'What are you going to do today?' she grinned.

'I dunno,' I replied. 'I can't think how to start. Hope you like the school.'

Bet slammed the front door and I heard her cheery 'Watcha' to some stranger in the street. I smiled to myself as I wondered what the neighbours would make of her cockney sound. Getting up, my feet touched bare boards. Unpacked tea chests and rolled-up carpets were cluttered around the room.

Over a cup of coffee, I pondered just how I should spend the day. It was so different from my first day at the Social Services office. Then I had been shown to a desk, introduced to colleagues, given files to read and told what families to visit. Here I had no office, no desk, no colleagues, no files and, as yet, knew hardly any families. I tried to recall those college lectures. I had been taught how to write court reports, how to take a distraught patient into mental hospital, how to assess if an old age pensioner was fit to stay in his own home. I had sat through lectures on Marx on social class, marks on children's bottoms and marks (black ones) for essays. But I could recall no lessons on how to start living on a council estate.

I reminded myself that my job was to help families and

12

youngsters and that my best bet was to involve them in suggesting ways to reach the objectives. My first task, then, had to be one of meeting with and talking to local people. After four cups of coffee, a wash and a shave, I determined on a course of action. I would hang about the shop and pick up local news and gossip: I would knock on doors in the area in order to meet as many people as possible: and I would hang about the streets as a means of making contact with youngsters.

At the shop I mentioned my thoughts to Red Moore.

'Good idea,' he approved, 'and stick up a notice to tell people you're here and what you're doing.'

He searched along a cluttered shelf and eventually found a felt-tipped pen and paper. As I considered what to write, I realized that my activities had no name or title. I christened it the Edgely Project and wrote

> Edgely Project
> 31 Muddiford Grove,
> Bob Laken is available to
> help families and children.

Some of the shoppers and shop assistants gathered round as I pinned up the notice.

'What's it for?' asked Clare, a blonde-haired, dark-rooted, middle-aged divorcee. I tried to explain about wanting to keep families together, to reduce delinquency and to help kids.

'Well, you should have come three years ago when my old man ran off with Dolly Leighton. Still, the kids could do with something to do around here.'

Other women agreed with Clare and a shopper commented, 'Yes, get those motor bikes off the streets, they're making me deaf.'

Toni, a tall brunette who worked part-time in the shop, dug Clare in the ribs as she read the notice.

'Oh, he's available is he. Well, we'll know what to do when we're lonely.'

13

I'd made a start. The shop was the hub of the neighbourhood. Red told me that people would come in four or five times a day instead of collecting their shopping in one go. They came for company, to talk, to joke. Red welcomed the community role the shop played. Within the shop, the chatter was orchestrated by the female assistants. Many of their remarks were bawdy, provocative or downright insulting. But they were also prepared to spend time chatting to the old folks, or waiting patiently as small children decided how to spend their pennies.

A few days after pinning up the notice, I received the attention of the women. As I walked into the shop, Toni was standing behind a pile of corned beef tins. The tins were not selling because of a scare about infected meat.

Suddenly, Toni appeared to slip and called out in agonized tones, 'Bob, Bob, come and help, I've got me boobs stuck in the meat tins.'

The audience of shoppers paused to see how I would react. I replied, 'Sorry Toni, I don't like touching bad meat.'

The women guffawed with laughter and even Toni conceded, 'All right, that's the last invitation you get from me.'

Later, Red told me that the incident had been my initiation test. I had passed! There developed a joking, bantering relationship with the shop people which was to hold me in good stead in the future. The shop proved a daily source of information and contacts.

At the same time I was exploring the streets and knocking on doors. Tramping the streets brought two hazards. Motor bikes – carrying one, two or three riders – were likely to shoot along the road, the pavement, or even to emerge through hedges. Then there were dogs. Edgely abounded in large dogs who paraded the streets, ransacked dustbins and terrorized strangers. As a newcomer, my appearance in the road was likely to be notified by hairy beasts snapping at my heels, running between my legs and jumping up to plant muddy paws on my duffle coat.

Bet advised me to look them straight in the eye and never to retreat. So, on one occasion, I knelt down to stare into

14

the wild eyes of a black mongrel in an attempt to make friends. The next moment I was flat on my back with the mongrel and two of his canine cronies walking all over me. A crowd of laughing kids looked on.

Sometimes the two hazards combined, for the dogs delighted in chasing motor bikes and the teenage riders specialized in missing the animals by as small a margin as possible.

Having developed antennae for spotting the approach of motor bikes or dogs, I got on with door-knocking. My method was to shove a letter explaining my job through the letter boxes and then call a couple of days later to see what residents had to say. The response was varied.

At one home, a few teenagers were playing records. Hearing my footsteps, a girl opened the window and shouted, 'If you're the b... welfare, Mum says I'm not at school 'cos I've got a cold.'

When I explained that I was not the welfare, the rent man or a plain clothes detective, they let me in and I met some youngsters whom I was to know closely in the following years.

At another house, my knock provoked a terrier to emerge from the back garden with the speed of a bullet. Equalling any Olympic hurdler, I leapt the garden fence as the dog's teeth actually closed on my trousers. As I sat on one side of the fence, eyeing the snarling jaws on the other, an elderly woman emerged.

'Did you knock? He won't hurt you. He's ever so friendly,' she yelled.

She invited me into the house, where my terror and humiliation soon faded as we chatted. Mrs Barnes was a widow, a long-serving resident of Edgely. Her own children were grown up and married and she warmed to my concern for the youngsters in the area. Even on this first meeting, I sensed that she would be the kind of woman to whom I could turn if I ever needed a bed for a child.

A few houses along, the door was opened by a middle-aged woman with a bubble-cut and heavy eye shadow. She had read my letter.

15

'Mrs Peters, is there anything in this area in general or you in particular need?' I asked in my innocence.

'Yes,' she retorted. 'A rich man about your age. Come in.'

'Well, I'm not rich but I'll come in.'

As I entered, I saw that Mrs Peters' smart personal appearance contrasted with that of her home. The worn lino was decorated with tea stains and holes. Peeling wallpaper bore a multitude of crayon marks, ink blots and scratches. Three boys sat watching the TV. One, about fourteen years old, with close-cropped hair, should have been at school.

'Jardine's got an ear ache,' said Mrs Peters as though reading my thoughts.

'Oh, bad luck,' I murmured – thinking to myself, 'I'm not surprised with that great ring hanging from his left lughole.'

The next boy, an eight-year-old called Troy, continued to pick his nose as he focussed on play school. The third, Danny, a half-coloured boy of two, was wearing nothing but a short vest. A damp nappy was at his feet. He was the only child to take any notice of me but I wished he hadn't as he plonked a wet backside onto my lap and addressed me as 'dad'.

'Come out here and I'll give yer a cup of tea,' Mrs Peters bellowed from the kitchen. With Danny still clinging to me, I accepted her offer. Holding a mug of tea, Daphne Peters questioned me about myself, my wife, my job. When I had finished, she indicated her approval.

'It's about time somethink was done about the kids around here. I've had enough people call. Probation Officers, attendance lady, health visitor, district nurse, the welfare, and I still live in a pigsty with damp walls. So let's do it for the kids.'

'Would your husband have the time to help if I started something for the youngsters?' I asked, as a polite way of finding out about the father of the young Peters.

'*Have* time – he's doing time,' snorted Mrs Peters. 'Anyway, he won't be coming back here. He was useless, couldn't even do a break-in properly. Do you know how he got done last time? Stood outside the house next door, looking in with a pair of binoculars. Course, when their colour TV went missing they guessed straight away he did it. He's doing five years. Anyway, he won't come back now, not since I've had Danny.'

'Is Danny's dad here, then?' I casually enquired.

'Sometimes. More often he's not. We have a lot of rows. I'm not his only woman. He's got another one – his own colour – in town. I chased him with a carving knife when I first found out. What a night that was. We were in bed when he started boasting about her. I chased him naked into the garden. Calls himself a man. He hid in the coal shed. All the neighbours stared out of their windows, their eyes popping out of their heads. They phoned for the police. He was lucky. If I'd have caught him he wouldn't have had any more women. Can't stand a man who's not faithful.'

My eyes fell on the faded photo of another boy. Daphne Peters saw my interest and explained.

'Ah, that's my Phil. He's in Borstal. Doesn't know his own strength, that's his trouble. Pity you weren't here before. He was always bored, never knew what to do with himself and he'd end up smashing somethink or somebody.'

Mrs Peters then poured out her life story, her struggles, her poverty, her men, her illnesses.

As she put it, 'Life has dealt me many bad cards.' But she was still clinging to the hope that she would receive a better hand.

When I departed after two hours, it was with a grudging sense of admiration that she had survived and somehow managed to keep three of her sons with her.

Some of the homes I visited were warm, tidy, neat and comfortable inside. Others were cold, empty and bare. Mrs Battle's was in between. It was so full of furniture, the doors could not open fully, and I had to squeeze into each room. A film of dust was everywhere.

Eleanor Battle wore a turban of the kind popularized by female factory workers in the second world war. From the corner of her mouth drooped a fag which sprayed ash over a sagging jumper and crumpled skirt. On her feet were holey slippers in which she shuffled around, indoors and out.

17

As she invited me to sit down, I glanced round, noticing the books on the shelves and comics and magazines scattered all around. A closer look revealed such titles as *Vultures Today, Frankenstein Lives, Dracula Strikes* . . .

'It's the 'orrors,' explained Mrs Battle. 'The boys love their 'orrors.'

She then insisted on making some tea and brought in a plate of cakes. They too were covered in their share of the dust. Not disturbed, I confidently picked one up.

I thought to myself, 'One thing four years with the local authority did teach me was how to deal with unwelcome cakes.'

As soon as Mrs Battle left the room, I placed the cake on the floor and summoned a spaniel who had so far not stirred from his basket. He ambled over and I smirked at the memory of previous ravenous pets gobbling up unwanted morsels. But the dog sniffed the cake, turned it over, licked it – and left it. He waddled back to his slumbers. To my horror, I heard Mrs Battle's returning footsteps. I hastily snatched up the cake, tried to force it into my coat pocket, failed because they were full of leaflets and, as she opened the door, forced myself to take a bite.

'Have another,' she urged.

'No thanks, been eating all morning,' I mumbled, trying hard not to think about the spaniel's slimy tongue.

The dog-rejected cake was washed down with three cups of tea. Mrs Battle began to wax eloquent about herself and her family. I had already met her husband, a mild, elderly man who worked for the Gas Company and had fitted our cooker. His eyes bore a perpetual pained look and I now wondered if this was due to his wife. The name should be Bottle, not Battle, I thought – to judge by her breath and the flask of whisky behind a cushion. But Battle was also appropriate. Her sons Syd, aged 16, Fred (known as Fangs), 13, and Johnson, 9, all received the rough edge of her tongue. And, she was well known for her readiness to give verbal blows to anyone who crossed her path. At the same time, as she soon informed me, she did much to help the elderly housebound in the neighbourhood. I concluded that she would make a doughty friend but a destructive foe.

And so the visits went on. For three months I tramped the streets. The weather turned cold; snow came in November. I kept on knocking. By the end of the year, I was probably known to, and knew, over 100 people. I had learned something about the area – the high number of one-parent families and the plight of elderly people living alone. I listened to complaints about the teenagers on their motor bikes and their vandalism. A few people dismissed me as a 'do gooder', or with the cynical remark that nothing ever got done in Edgely. More frequently, I was warmed by appreciative remarks that at least somebody was interested. I developed a friendly, chatting relationship with a number of grown-ups and children. Yet I still needed to convince them of my integrity and sincerity.

Then it happened.

The front door was banged repeatedly. A boy's voice shouted urgently, 'Bob, Bob, quick, hurry.'

It was Saturday morning and Bet and I were enjoying a leisurely breakfast as she amused me with tales of the antics of her infant class. I leapt to the door. Jardine, the fourteen-year-old member of the Peters family stood there.

'It's Don Plumb, his leg's hanging off. Do something.'

I raced after Jardine, down the narrow alley on to a piece of waste ground. Local lads used it for motor-bike scrambling. Jardine and Don had been tinkering with an old wreck of a Moped and as we ran Jardine shouted that the Moped had taken off and come down with its chain cutting into Don. As we arrived, Don was staggering to his feet. His leg was not exactly hanging off, but the chain had ripped into the back of his calf. As he lurched forward, bits of flesh rolled down his leg. Taking one look, I knew I had no time to get his parents. I shouted to Jardine to tell Mr and Mrs Plumb, shouldered the bulky Don and managed to ease him into the back of the mini. Within minutes we were at the Casualty Department of the local hospital.

The nurse at Reception was calm, not to say frosty. She

19

did not look at Don's injury but very slowly took details about his age, address and own doctor. She frowned and shook her head when Don described how the accident occurred and told us to wait our turn in the crowded casualty room.

Don was incredibly brave, although obviously in pain. Blood was trickling to the floor and small pieces of flesh were gathering on his boots.

I could stand it no longer and grabbed the arm of a passing nurse. 'Please look at this lad's leg.'

The nurse took one glance and immediately fetched a doctor. A mobile stretcher was summoned and within seconds two doctors and several nurses were cutting away Don's trousers, cleaning the wound and preparing him for an operation. Mr Plumb arrived at this juncture. Over six foot tall, a crane driver, athletic and strong, he was much respected on the estate. He took one look at the huge gap of a wound and almost threw up. He left the room in a hurry. I remained holding Don's hand. His dad soon returned. Within a short space of time, Don was on the operating table undergoing a skin graft.

A second operation followed. Bet and I went every day to see Don, sometimes taking local youngsters, until Troy Peters' antics on the hospital wheelchairs caused them to be banned. The graft was successful and Don suffered no permanent injury, except for a huge and unsightly scar.

Mr and Mrs Plumb expressed their thanks for my quick action. News of the accident spread – in a much exaggerated version given by Jardine. Parents spoke to me about it. Youngsters somehow thought I had saved Don's life, or personally given him a new leg.

The affair proved a breakthrough. It seemed to convince residents that I was genuine. People became more ready to express their problems, and the number of youngsters who knocked at our door began to increase.

2
Getting Started

It was 10.35 p.m. on a Saturday evening. We were just settling down to watch *Match of the Day* on TV. For once, West Ham were on. Bet and I were about to wallow in nostalgic memories of the days when we used to squeeze into the Upton Park soccer ground and there join in a chorus of 'I'm for ever blowing bubbles' with 20,000 East London nasal voices.

The door knocker hammered. I reluctantly raised myself from the armchair and opened the door.

Webster Summerfield stood there. His lip was cut. One tooth had been forced sideways so that it rested in front of another tooth. The skin under his left eye was red and bruised. Blood was trickling from the corner of his mouth. The sight was enough to drive even football from my mind. I took him in.

I had often met Webster on the street. About fourteen years old, he wore his hair long and possessed a nose broken in a fight or accident. Apart from that I knew little about him, just that he was being brought up by his mother. Mrs Summerfield was, to put it politely, a well-built woman with a reputation for being both aggressive and warm-hearted. We had conversed a few times but so far I felt she was still keeping me at a distance.

'Sorry to call so late,' spluttered Webster. 'I had nowhere else to go.'

Bet fetched warm water and cotton wool and we bathed his wounds. Webster gave his version of what had happened. Mum was out for the evening and he had made a meal for himself. His older brother, Flint, had returned full of beer but empty of food. Finding the larder bare, he had blamed Webster, beaten him up and kicked him out.

We patched Webster up and advised him to go to the dentist on Monday.

'Good, I'll miss school,' he grinned.

Then I went home with him. Mrs Summerfield was back. I explained briefly what had happened. Her lips tightened and she glared across the room at Flint.

'Get upstairs. I'll deal with you later. You're not too old for the belt.'

Mrs Summerfield was a redoubtable woman. Flint was over six foot tall, with muscles toughened by his work as a building labourer. Yet he slunk off to bed without a word – though his hostile glare at Webster said plenty. Sandra Summerfield thanked me and I left.

Webster's call was one of a growing number of knocks on the door as the new year began. In the back garden, we had put up a swing ball which acted like a magnet. The garden sided on to a road and soon youngsters were climbing the fence to play. Thanks to a nearby street lamp they could even enjoy floodlit swing ball. They played until late at night, even when snow was on the ground. The older ones began to drop in for a coffee and a chat.

One evening a deputation of about fifteen asked if they could see me. I invited them in and put on the kettle. They came straight to the point.

'What about a youth club?' The spokesman was Jardine Peters.

'There's nothin' to do round here. You've only got to open yer mouth in the street and people start moaning,' added Syd Battle. Syd, a plump sixteen-year-old, wore tight-fitting blue jeans, a waistcoat and ear-rings. His brother, Fangs – so named because of two huge front teeth – grunted his agreement.

Fiona Scott, a vivacious, quietly spoken teenager with shoulder-length auburn hair, informed us that Dylan Willis, a young married man, had said he would be prepared to help with a club. I made a mental note to visit him.

Legs Lancing, a seventeen-year-old with black greasy hair

and a black leather jacket unravelled himself from the clutches of his adoring girl friend, Ruby Curtis. The strap of his crash helmet had somehow got entangled around the belts of both their jeans. He calmly undid the belts. No one sniggered, for he was obviously held in some awe if not fear. I was expecting a great speech after the cool and deliberate build-up but he just said, 'I'll help as well,' and returned to cuddling Ruby.

Drew Sprite, a ten-year-old who should have been in bed, succeeded in knocking over three cups of coffee.

Diversions apart, a high level of interest and enthusiasm was maintained. Eventually, at my suggestion, a small committee was formed. It was agreed to invite Dylan Willis to be chairman while I accepted the task of finding somewhere to hold the club.

The following day, I called on Dylan Willis. He welcomed me enthusiastically. A twenty-eight-year-old labourer, he was married to a petite and charming wife, Doreen, and had one child, nine-year-old Rebecca. Born and bred in Edgely, Dylan had seen an older brother sent to approved school and prison. His concern for local youngsters seemed to stem from a desire to stop them going the same way. Tall, witty and a karate expert, he seemed ideal material for involvement in the youth club.

Finding premises was not so easy. Charlie Wantage energetically thumbed through his diary, only to find that the church hall was booked up. The secretary of another church hall said that their previous attempt to start a youth club had produced such noise and damage by the youngsters that it had been decided never to let them in again. When I approached the schools I was told that any applications had to go through County Hall some twenty miles away and that, in any case, staff were not keen to have their polished floors scratched by the youth of Edgely.

Apart from church halls and schools, I knew of no other premises in the locality. The youth club looked like folding up before it had even started. Then one lunch-time, as I strolled along the trunk road which skirted the estate, I saw

23

a number of schoolboys furtively peering into the windows of an old prefab. It was one of two prefabs which stood opposite the comprehensive school and I had taken them to be a part of it. I now noticed a small sign which read LABOUR'S STUDIOS. The thought of hiring them for the club crossed my mind. I walked in and saw at once the reason for the schoolboys' interest. Perched on a high stool sat a female model clothed only in goose pimples and 'warmed' by a small electric fire. My reaction was one of pity that anyone had to sit naked on such a cold day. Around her, trying hard to transfer the model's shapely form on to paper, were four art students – three middle-aged ladies and one elderly man.

'Can I help you? I'm Labour.'

The question was put by the studio's owner, a tall thin figure whose beard was as wide, and almost as long, as his body. So Labour's Studios did not, as I had imagined, mean that they belonged to the Labour Party. Mr Lew Labour regarded me as a potential recruit to his art classes. I declined. I can hardly draw matchstick men! Not offended, Mr Labour called for a lunch break, threw a blanket to his shivering model and invited me to join them for soup.

As we sat around the two-barred electric fire, warming our hands against the mugs of soup, Lew explained his activities. He had come to Edgely with a vision of bringing art to the working classes. Fortunate enough to rent the two surplus prefab classrooms from the Education Authority, he had dreamt of introducing both children and adults to the creative joys of painting. Unfortunately, the working classes had not responded and his tuition group never contained more than a handful of pupils. Even this was threatened as the head-master of the school was annoyed at the anatomical interest displayed by his pupils during the lunch hours. On the bright side, Lew's own paintings were finding a market in the cafés and craft shops in the town centre, so he reckoned he could survive even without his classes.

Once lunch was over, the model grabbed the electric fire and resumed her pose. Lew moved amongst his adoring pupils giving words of advice. He returned to me and plied

24

me with questions about my work. He seemed sympathetic and I took the opportunity to ask if I could hire one of the prefabs for the youth club. He responded positively and we went to look at the other hut. It was even colder than the first. An old-fashioned boiler was intended to supply heat, although Lew admitted that he had never lit it. The schoolroom floor was uneven and damp. Nonetheless, we agreed a modest fee and the Edgely Youth Club had a home.

The club opened in February. About forty teenagers attended. Dylan Willis kept his promise to come and – with his good humour and expertise in games – proved a great help. Jardine Peters collected the entrance fees. Fangs and Syd Battle had rescued an old table tennis top from a rubbish dump and placed it on four school desks which had been left in the prefab. Legs Lancing brought along his 'bullworker' so that members could build up their muscles. Don Plumb, his leg still in plaster, lent his record player and served as our resident D.J. I had used part of the project's meagre funds to purchase a second-hand snooker table. Maureen and Mo Moore came along with a supply of paper cups, coffee and sugar kindly donated by their parents. Fiona Scott supplied some board games, including monopoly. Gail, Ruby and Lesley did not bring any goods but contributed their high spirits and a readiness to take to the floor and dance.

Webster Summerfield had taken charge of the 'café' at the club. It was no more than a table in a corner. The sweets, crisps and bottles of coke were kept on chairs against the wall, as Webster said they would be nicked if members could reach them. I'm not sure how he became the café manager. He just took the job on and proceeded to do it very well. His ready wit soon attracted customers. He reminded me of the barrow boys I had once known in the markets of East London.

Despite his success, Webster was not popular with other members. Perhaps they resented his jealously guarded position behind the counter. Hints were dropped that some of the takings went into his pocket. Another worrying point was his quick temper. Members only had to jog the table or grumble at the service and he would flare up.

The boiler proved difficult to light and, when at last I got it going, belched out foul clouds of smoke. Its pipes – which ran along the walls and across the ceiling – began to drip water. The room was cold and bare. Our equipment was inadequate. But, all in all, the evening passed successfully and the members were enthusiastic. At the close, a number volunteered to stay behind and clear up. The only disappointment for me was discovering, when everyone had gone, that toilet rolls had been stuffed down the loos and graffiti scrawled across the lavatory walls.

As the weeks went by the need to order new stock for the café made Webster a frequent caller at our house. The visits became daily and before long Bet was commenting on the special kind of relationship that had developed between us. He rarely stayed in his own home. Sometimes he walked into the town centre to play the machines in the arcade – which prompted the uneasy question of where the cash came from; I knew he received little from his mum. Apart from this, Webster spent hours in the local streets.

Perhaps it was the cold, or the loneliness, or the need for friendship, but something drove him to seek my company. We spent hours talking over coffee or watching TV. Initially, he would discuss in great detail his problems at school. His exercise books showed that he was backward academically, yet I knew from the rapid way he added up the café money that he possessed basic mathematical skills. His lack of progress was probably due more to his inability to get on with any adults who wielded authority. Every day, it seemed, he was in some scrape at school.

At first, I couldn't help laughing at his vividly recounted tales of how he enraged teachers by pressing the fire bell, or how he replaced the staff-room sugar with salt. Then it dawned on me that his behaviour was more serious than boyish pranks. When a female teacher reprimanded him for tattooing his arm with a compass point and ink – a popular

26

practice at the time – he called her a tart and stormed from the classroom.

One afternoon Webster arrived at my door.

'What are you doing home at this hour?' I asked.

'Oh, they let us out early.'

'Come off it, it's only half past two.'

'Well, I've been suspended. It's that rat Simpson. He complained to the head just because I was sitting on the dustbins.'

Webster had a knack of describing the deeds for which he was punished in so slighting a fashion that the listener tended to assume he had been dealt with too harshly. But I knew him by now. Webster had a running feud with 'Simple' Simpson, the caretaker. On this occasion, I later discovered, Webster had been hiding behind the dustbins having a quiet drag. The caretaker, coming to move the dustbins, had told Webster to get out. He refused and the verbal slanging match degenerated into a scuffle, egged on by cheering boys. Mr Simpson then stormed into the headmaster's study and complained that Webster had attacked him. Either Webster Summerfield went, or he did.

The upshot was that Webster was suspended for a week while the school decided what to do. During that week I talked with Webster about his reactions to people who tried to discipline him. We went over the incidents which resulted in the blow-ups. I produced pen and paper and we drew the scenes as cartoons. He produced an amusing picture of his mum brandishing her belt and one of me when I had clipped him round the ear for bullying a younger child. I drew matchstick men scenes of him 'blowing up' at school.

'See, you don't always have a fit when you get told off,' I said as we compared the pictures.

'That's different,' he replied. 'I like mum and you. I don't like caretakers and teachers.'

'Right. So your next step is to learn to live with people you don't like. OK?'

'Suppose so.'

Eventually, at Mrs Summerfield's request, I accompanied

her and Webster when they went to see the headmaster. Faced with the head, the deputy head, the head of year and his form teacher, Webster was unusually silent. But Sandra Summerfield waxed strong in his defence. Too much so, for I could see the teachers' irritation rising as she switched from defence to attack.

'He does what I tell him or he knows what he gets. You can't handle him. You've no discipline. And you pick on him, just like you did on his brother. And what's he learning? Nothing.'

The discourse was beginning to degenerate into argument, with me sitting uneasily on the fence, when Webster broke in.

'All right, all right, I'm sorry. Bob and I had a talk about it and I want to go and see old "Simple" and apologize.'

The teachers were pleased to find a way out of their dilemma, one which might stop the flow of accusations from Mrs Summerfield and yet also satisfy the caretaker. Webster departed to find Mr Simpson. He reported to me later that his old enemy was so surprised at the apology that he became quite friendly. The suspension was lifted. The immediate difficulty was over but I did not kid myself it would not recur.

The following Sunday, Bet and I went for a walk and some local kids trailed along with us. Within half an hour we were away from the rows of houses and out among the muddy green hills of the surrounding countryside. We made for Steam Tunnel, a mile-long railway tunnel, now disused. The smaller youngsters enjoyed the tunnel, particularly in the middle where the darkness completely enveloped us. As we reached the end and emerged into the wintry sunshine, Webster fell into step beside me.

'Been thinking.'

'Makes a change,' I grinned. 'What about?'

Webster hesitated. He flicked his long brown hair out of his eyes and sniffed. The skin on his forehead creased as he struggled for words.

'You know when you went with mum and me to the school

28

– well, it was like I had a dad again.' He looked down at his feet.

My heart jumped, as a curious mixture of emotions surged over me. Elation at his confidence in me. Sadness that a boy of his age should have no father to turn to. Fear that he was trying to cast me in a role I could never fulfill. How many of Webster's difficulties, his lack of control, his explosiveness, perhaps his stealing, were connected with the absence of a dad?

'Webster, you've never talked to me about your dad. What happened to him? Do you still see him?'

'He walked out when I was seven,' replied Webster, his lips curling. 'He was never in much anyway. He and mum were always rowing. But I didn't want him to go. When he said he was leaving, I begged him to stay. He just said, "Get out of the way, you little bugger." "Little bugger", that's what he thought of me. He never liked me. He might have stayed if he'd liked me.'

The other children had wandered away with Bet. I could hear their laughter coming from the banks of the old railway line.

'Do you ever seen him now?' I asked gently.

'Now and then we bump into each other. He's living with a tart in Blackway. And he's got more children. Last time we bumped into each other he just said "hello" and walked away. I heard his kids ask who I was and he just said he knew my mum. Knew my mum, that's all.'

I put my hand on his shoulder. We stopped walking and I looked him in the eyes.

'Webster, I can't take the place of your dad. But you know you can turn to me. Our door is always open to you.'

Webster turned away. His eyes were full of tears. I was not sure if they were tears of delight or tears of disappointment.

The establishment of the youth club pleased parents as well as youngsters. People find it hard to understand what social workers do but the formation of a club was something concrete which obviously benefited their children. Consequently, even more people started greeting me and stopped to talk in the street. The readiness to chat was not confined to youth club matters.

Toni drew me aside in the shop to ask how she and her husband could adopt a child.

Red Moore suggested I kept an eye on a dad who was walloping his son.

Then one morning, as I was strolling towards the shop, a window shot up and Clare Curtis shouted to me to come in. She shoved a mug of tea in front of me and carried on removing curlers from her hair. Gail, Ruby and Lesley were rushing around stuffing toast into their mouths and looking for school books. They were lively, cheeky girls.

'Hello Bob, you're up early. Didn't Bet fancy you this morning?'

'Watch our mum, she'll attack you with her curlers.'

'We're going now. Is it safe to leave you two together?'

Clare landed her foot up the backside of the nearest Curtis as they disappeared out of the door.

'Sorry, Bob, they get out of hand sometimes.'

'Oh, they just like a bit of fun,' I replied. 'They've been a great help at club. They're quite the centre of attraction with their dancing.'

'Um, that's OK then. But I don't want them to get too flirty. Young girls these days go too far too soon. Anyway, I didn't ask you in to talk about them. What do you think about this?'

Clare pointed a painted finger-nail at an advertisement which she had ringed in the local paper. It was for a lunch-time barmaid in town. The problem was that Clare was drawing social security. She wondered if she would be in trouble if she started earning as well. Fortunately, I knew the answer and explained that she was allowed to earn a limited amount, even while receiving money from the state. Clare brightened.

'That's a relief to know. I'll ring up. I've always fancied myself as a barmaid.' She paused. 'Thanks, Bob. Look, I wonder if you'd do something for a friend of mind, Blondie Blake. She's really depressed about the damp in her flat. It's disgraceful. She's got small kids.'

Clare's words were my introduction to Blondie. She was to figure large in my life during the following years.

Blondie lived in one of the few flats in Edgely. It was the top flat of a five-storey matchbox-type building. There were no lifts, so I climbed the stairs and rang the bell. No reply. A baby was crying. I pressed again. Still no reply. I banged hard on the knocker. A voice yelled at the baby to shut up. At last the door opened a fraction. I explained that Clare had asked me to call.

'Oh,' grunted Blondie, 'I thought you were that TV rent man again. Come in.'

I followed Blondie as she shuffled into the kitchen. She was in her early twenties. Uncombed, blonde hair cascaded around her shoulders. Dark brown eyes, a prominent nose and a wide mouth combined to produce not a beautiful but certainly a striking face. Her slouching gait, tea-stained jumper and shabby skirt did not hide the shapely figure. She shouted again at the kids to belt up. June, aged eighteen months, crawled around the lino, whining to be picked up. Wally, aged seven, immediately asked, 'Are you my dad?'

My instant enthusiasm to kneel down and make friends with him was dampened by Blondie's comment that he was home from school because she thought he had dysentery.

I glanced out of the kitchen window and was about to comment on the fine view it gave over Edgely.

'Don't look out there, look up here,' snapped Blondie. She pointed to the ceiling. A wet patch some five feet across was turning to mould. Fungus was growing above the window top.

'You should see it when it rains. It pours in,' she added.

'Haven't you got on to the council?' I asked.

'The council. They've mended it twice. Made it worse. What's the use. I give up.'

She slouched over to the cooker and put the kettle on. She beckoned me to look into the bedrooms. One was so damp that she had vacated it and she and the children were sleeping in one room.

'Blondie, this is terrible. We're going to the council today.'

31

'You mean, you'll come with me?'

'Of course.'

Blondie brightened considerably. We sat down and she began to tell me about herself as we sipped tea. Illegitimate, her mother abandoned her when she was five. She then lived with an old woman, known as 'gran', until the old woman died. At ten, Blondie was taken into care and passed from one children's home to another. At sixteen, she moved into a working girls' hostel. At seventeen, she married a rugged Scotsman who drove long-distance lorries from the north. She stayed with him in Glasgow for six months, became pregnant, left him and moved back to Edgely, where Wally was born. She had another child – who was placed for adoption by an Irishman, a miscarriage by a Welshman, and June was the result of a casual affair with an Englishman.

'See, I'm not prejudiced,' she giggled. Blondie showed no embarrassment in talking about her affairs, adding that her latest bloke was a sailor who stayed at weekends.

Blondie stretched out on the settee, thrusting her legs over its back so that her skirt pushed up to reveal her thighs. She grinned and went on, 'But don't get the wrong idea about me. I only go with one bloke at a time and I don't do it for money.'

Suddenly she was on her feet and clouting Wally round his ear. Unnoticed by us, he had been picking bits off the wallpaper.

'Pick, pick, pick, that's all he does. He's nuts,' exploded Blondie.

I sat Wally down beside me and persuaded him to do some drawings. The way Blondie behaved, I thought to myself, it wasn't surprising that Wally resorted to peeling off the wallpaper.

Within a few hours, I had made an appointment and took Blondie to the housing department. A neighbour had agreed to keep an eye on Wally and June. The receptionist obviously recognized Blondie for she motioned her to sit, made a phone call, and then directed us to a cubicle. After a few minutes, a tall, thin bespectacled man walked in.

'You again, Mrs Blake. I've told you before, we can't

re-house you with rent arrears.' Turning to me, he added, 'If you are living there, I hope you've informed social security. It's an offence to cohabit with a woman who is claiming support for herself and her children.'

Blondie guffawed and put her arms round me.

'Cor, this is quick, even for me. I only met him this morning.'

I felt my face burning as I removed her hands. I introduced myself and pointed out that I had phoned earlier. The official rose and left. After a short wait, a middle-aged, portly man in grey flannels and sports jacket appeared.

'I'm Ridgway, divisional area manager. Sorry about the muddle. Your message wasn't passed on.'

Although we were now treated with respect, even kindness, the message was the same. The housing department was short-staffed and it would be weeks before they could attempt to tackle the problems of damp. Further, Blondie was in arrears with the rent, and the council rule was that debtors could not be transferred to other property.

'I knew it,' Blondie burst out as we left. 'They don't want to help. They know I can't get the money.'

'Come off it, Blondie. He's got to keep the rules. But we're not finished yet.'

We then made two more calls. Blondie's doctor was a ginger-haired young practitioner in his first year of general practice. Fortunately, Dr Keen had already heard about me from the Rev. Wantage. Although he was about to go off duty, he readily came to the flat and agreed to write to the Housing Department informing them that the dampness was detrimental to the health of the children. He also instructed Blondie to bring Wally to the surgery that evening.

Considerably heartened, Blondie and I then proceeded to the social security office. I was prepared to donate half the amount from our funds if the social security would make an emergency payment of the rest to cover the rent arrears. In view of Dr Keen's comments, I argued that the health dangers did constitute an emergency. Somewhat to my surprise, the official agreed on the spot.

The following day, the rent arrears were paid off. Dr

Keen's letter soon followed. A week later, Bet and I were piling up the week's groceries in the shop when Blondie burst in, waving a letter.

'We've done it,' she shouted. 'They're moving me to a new house.'

The children, too young to understand, caught her mood. Wally grabbed a shopping trolley and charged around in circles. June jumped up and down until, in her excitement, she wet herself and wee-d in a corner – appropriately over some leeks.

The starting of the club, the friendship with Webster, the rehousing of Blondie, were seen as successes. I began to get big-headed, thinking I was the walking answer to Edgely's problems. Then, within a few days, it all crumbled.

One week, numbers doubled at the club. Word had got round and a bunch of youngsters from Blackway – the council estate about two miles from Edgely – arrived. Solidarity, friendship and unity, they had said at college, were the hallmarks of the working class. Things must have changed since those lectures. The Edgely and Blackway lads kept apart but shouted obscenities and insults at each other. The whole evening was tense, as Dylan and I tried to mix with both sets.

Eventually, Ruby Curtis complained to Legs Lancing that one of the opposition had 'touched her up'. Legs immediately grabbed the offender and proceeded to lay into him with his size ten Dr Martyn boots. The place was in an uproar as the kids crowded round and other skirmishes developed.

It was Dylan Willis who saved the day. He pulled Legs off his opponent and held them apart. Both lads respected and feared Dylan too much to try and hit him. Dylan motioned for the record player to be turned off and shouted to the crowd to listen to me. I had not anticipated making a speech but I bluntly told them that if they wanted to get us booted out they were going the right way about it. The tension eased and most of the Blackway crowd left.

The local youngsters tried to cajole me into banning outsiders saying that the club was only for Edgely. I replied –

rather weakly – that the committee must decide. Worse, when we cleared up at the end, the loos were again crammed with toilet rolls and coke bottles, a billiard cue had been snapped in two, and the outside door was torn from its hinges.

I began to wonder if the club was worth the trouble.

The very next day, I suffered the first hints of local criticism. Mrs Battle stopped me in the shop and said she thought I should know that some people were saying I had favourites.

'Favourites!' I exclaimed. 'What do you mean?'

'Some people thing you give too much time to them that don't deserve it and too little to them that do.'

I understood. I was devoting attention to kids like Webster Summerfield and not to her children. I tried to explain that often the most unpopular children were those who needed most help. Mrs Battle snorted.

'Oh, I'm not talking about anyone in particular. It's just that I thought you ought to know what people are saying.'

That evening, Fangs and Syd Battle, Gail Curtis and Jules Thomas came to complain that Webster was fiddling the money at the club café. I was disappointed at the possibility, although not altogether surprised. More worrying was the division appearing between club members. And I could not think how to raise the matter with Webster without giving the impression that I believed he was a thief. After the four departed, I was left with a sick feeling in the pit of my stomach and the sure knowledge of trouble ahead.

Things weren't just going wrong with the club members. Blondie's bubble also burst. The day she moved into her new house, it snowed and the removal lorry got stuck. When she finally arrived, the gas had not been connected. She reached a call-box and late in the evening tearfully informed me that the house was freezing, she had no power for the gas cooker, the kids were starving and June would not stop screaming. I managed to borrow a couple of electric fires and a cooking-ring. By 11 p.m. Blondie and the kids were warm, fed and watered.

After seeing to Blondie, I staggered home and into bed.

At 12 o'clock the door knocker was hammered. It was Lionel again. His landlord had locked him out. Lionel wanted to stay with me but I insisted on accompanying him back to his digs. After persistent knocking, Mr Finch opened the door. He started to explain that Lionel kept coming in so late and so noisily that his children were woken up. In order to teach him a lesson, Mr Finch had locked him out. Lionel retorted that Mr Finch was stealing from his bedroom. The landlord angrily denied the charge and accused Lionel of peeing on the stairs. By this time they were both indoors, so I left them to it.

It was one in the morning when I returned. Bet had got up and had some hot cocoa on the boil. We sat and looked around the living-room. The walls were still bare. Working all hours, I'd had no time even to put up wallpaper. Ice was forming inside the windows and, as we spoke, our misty breath could be seen. At least the floor had a new carpet on it. New, but it bore a huge ink-stain where Danny Peters had managed to knock over a bottle of blue-black. I felt cold, tired and defeated. I was not looking after Bet in the way I should. My despair was all the more intense, coming so soon after my earlier feelings of elation.

I could have packed the job in there and then.

'Let's go for a walk,' Bet suggested.

I looked at her, wondering if the late nights had turned her brain.

'It's nearly half past one,' I protested.

'I know. And it's so still and calm outside. Anyway it's probably warmer than in here.'

My initial amazement gave place to a warm feeling of love. I knew Bet was tired. I knew she wanted a neater and tidier home. Yet here she was, thinking of me again.

So we went for the walk. And it was beautiful. The frost had cast icy patterns on the hedges, the windows and the rooftops. Edgely was at peace. We hardly spoke, just held hands and walked. Venturing past the council estate and into the short roads bounded by terraced Victorian houses, we came across a small building. I had not noticed it before. It was a tiny, non-conformist chapel, not much bigger than a one-car garage. The walls were made of breeze block, the roof of tin. A notice on the wall said:

Ebenezer Independent Chapel
If you think the church is made up
of hypocrites, come inside.
We've room for one more.

We grinned and somehow felt cheered.

As well as our love for each other, Bet and I were borne up by our faith. If we did not talk much about our beliefs, they were not diminished by that. Neither of us came from Christian homes. However, the youth club leader – whom I admired very much – had been a Christian and I had warmed to his beliefs. Later, as an adult, I read the Bible and became completely hooked on the person of Jesus Christ. His calm and peace in the midst of a life of pressures, trials and betrayal impressed me. I became a Christian – determined to follow him. While at college, Bet too placed her trust in Christ. We did not belong to any one denomination but were happy to worship anywhere.

That winter morning, as we trudged home, we determined to visit that chapel. When we reached home, fresh cups of cocoa in our hands, we looked out of the window and prayed together. That was what gave us the strength to continue.

3
Meet the People

Mr Plumb came charging along the field. His hobnail boots pounded on the turf. His wide girth required both a huge belt and braces to support his trousers. Sweating profusely, he gradually drew level with Drew Sprite and then overtook him. Once past the winning tape, he held his hands aloft as though he had won an Olympic medal. Don Plumb, still limping but with his leg out of plaster, rushed over to congratulate his dad. Drew muttered that he would have won if he hadn't slipped. His mum consoled him by saying it wasn't fair for men to compete against boys.

It was Spring. I had been in Edgely for seven months. After the night we stumbled across Ebenezer Chapel, I had sought out the man who ran it. Ted Williams was a window cleaner. Short and squat, he had long arms, small legs and a wide grin. He explained that the chapel had been unused and almost ruined. He had rebuilt it with his own labour. Now he and his wife, Roly, ran an informal Sunday School and evening service. He was deeply, even passionately, concerned about the quality of family life on the estate.

'God sent his Son to earth as a member of a family,' he argued. 'The family *must* be important. Bob, do something to bring families together.'

I accepted his suggestion and when the bitter winter gave way to a sparkling May, I organized a Parents v Youngsters Sports Day. There were no fields on the estate, so we had to hold the event on the nearest open space, an oval-shaped field in the middle of Blackway Estate. The agreed date was the Spring Bank Holiday which happened to be blessed with fine weather. Families brought sandwiches and Red Moore supplied a tank of orange squash. Even some of the old folk like Mrs Barnes and Mr Blenkinsop arrived to enjoy the sun and the fun.

Dylan and Doreen Willis proved the star performers for the parents. Tall and athletic, they won grudging respect from the teenagers whom they trounced in the sprints.

Clare Curtis and Blondie Blake looked fit in their brief shorts but tended to run with toes turned and knees knocking. They were easily outpaced by the fleet-footed Moore and Curtis girls.

The jumping events produced the most laughs. Mrs Battle, clad in a smelly jumper, ankle-length skirt and football socks, somehow ended her high jump attempt with the pole stuck under her skirt and jutting out of the neck of the jumper.

Webster refused to participate, saying it was too hot. He was content to be in charge of the drinks.

As the day moved to a close, I found myself sitting next to Mrs Peters. She plonked young Danny on my lap and he proceeded to run sticky fingers down my shirt.

'Good. I wanted a chance to speak to you, Bob. You know my Phil's in Borstal. I'm dead worried about him. He hasn't written for weeks. Last time I went there, he hardly spoke a word. Would you go and see him? I've told him all about you.'

Dylan, sitting nearby, overhead our conversation.

'I'd like to go with you,' he said, 'I used to knock around with Phil in the old days.'

So it was agreed we should go. Meanwhile the sports had finished. Dylan walked back with the youngsters in order to forestall any trouble with the Blackway boys. I ferried some of the parents back in the mini-van. As Mrs Plumb got out, she turned round and said, 'Bob, that's the first time we in Edgely have done something together.'

Together. That word stuck in my mind. It was the same word used by Ted Williams.

Two weeks later, Dylan and I arrived outside Dryden Borstal. No barbed wire or iron bars encircled the place. Just a brick wall and wooden gate. A gruff, uniformed official – who called me 'sir' in a tone which emphasized his own superiority – examined our visiting order and ushered us through. Following his instructions, we parked the van. His advice still rang in our ears.

'Lock your petrol cap, sir. The inmates think it funny to put sugar in visitors' petrol tanks.'

The Borstal, as far as I could see, consisted of prefabricated huts, gravel paths, green fields and vegetable gardens. Young men in grey overalls were tending the plants. Every now and then, a stream of burly youngsters, clad in long, grey shorts and with cropped hair, trotted by as even burlier instructors hurled orders and abuse at them. Keeping out of the runners' path, we walked to Hut A and entered, as instructed, by door V. Once inside, we stood in a narrow corridor until a grill opened and a hand was held out.

'Do we shake it or kiss it?' grinned Dylan.

I placed the visiting order in the hand and, after a few moments, a disembodied voice told us to proceed through door 3. Door 3 opened to an empty room furnished with small tables, hard chairs and highly polished brown lino. We sat down and waited.

After five minutes, the door opened and a man with thinning hair stepped in.

'Phil Peters?' I asked, thinking to myself that if Borstal had aged him, it did at least allow him to wear a neat, black suit.

'I'm Gregory the Welfare Officer,' he replied, choosing to ignore my apparent insult. 'Thought I'd see you, as I believe you've never met Peters before and I want to put you in the picture.'

Mr Gregory paused. He obviously regarded me as an inexperienced do-gooder who was sticking his nose into something he could not handle.

'I know Peters,' he went on. 'I know his type. He's got violent tendencies. He's already been in trouble for assaulting a member of staff. He needs a firm hand. I make a point of not giving him any privileges unless he works for them. That's how I've earned his respect. I strongly advise you to do the same. We don't want these soft "it's all in the relationship" theories which you college people are bringing into social work.'

Having delivered his lecture, Mr Gregory departed and, after a few minutes, Phil at last entered. Nearly six foot tall, broad and strong looking, he appeared the picture of health. I introduced myself and his eyes lit up as he recognized Dylan. Soon they were laughing about old times. As they chatted, I observed that, for all his glowing health, Phil was becoming like an old lag. He tended to talk out of the side of his mouth, he kept shooting glances at the door and, when Dylan offered him a cigarette, he took two extra for later on.

After a while, Phil turned to me.

'The old dear seems to have taken to you. She wrote and told me all about you. I thought you were her latest fancy man. Then she explained you were a social worker. Hope you're not like old Gregory, can't stand him. Still, mum says you're all right. Do you think you can get me a job when I get out of here?'

I replied that I could but try. I had a sinking feeling that Mrs Peters had given her son the impression that I would be able to solve all his problems. As I listened to his boasting about his fights with other inmates, his successful conning of Mr Gregory and his determination to make life awkward for the 'screws', I began to doubt if anyone could help him.

After an hour, our time was up. As we made our farewells, Phil asked if I'd send him some magazines.

'Sure,' I replied, glad to encourage his literary pursuits, 'what do you want?'

'*The Shooting Times*, it's all about country life, hunting, guns – one of my big interests.'

'Oh yes, and I can imagine what Mr Gregory would say if I sent that.'

'Come again,' yelled Phil, as we departed through the door.

On the return journey, we stopped at a motorway café. Munching a piece of plastic fruit cake, Dylan started telling me about local reactions to Bet and myself.

'The boys like Bet's legs and your cups of coffee,' Dylan observed with a twinkle in his eye. I nodded, pointing out

41

that I appreciated both myself. Apparently most people thought we were genuine, but a few reckoned we would move away after a few months.

'I'm sure you're good for Edgely,' Dylan went on, more seriously, 'and in a way I feel strongly that I want to be a part of what you are doing. But there's a question I must ask. Why do you do it? Why have you come?'

I paused. I went to purchase another coffee as I considered my reply. I tried to convey to Dylan that there was no single or simple reason. My motives stemmed from a dissatisfaction with my previous job, a vague desire to contribute to a better society, a wish to develop a more effective form of social work and a conviction that somehow I had been led into the job by a force, a spiritual force, greater than myself.

'I believe God led me here,' I said.

I thought my words might puzzle Dylan. Far from it.

'I know what you mean,' he responded. 'It's funny seeing Phil after all this time. He reminds me of what I was like. My brother went to Borstal. I admired him and reckon I was going the same way. Then I chummed up with a chap called Williams. I was about sixteen. It was difficult to talk to my dad but easy to talk to him. We had a common liking for dogs and used to walk them together in the country. He kind of told parables, although I didn't realize it straight away. He explained what happened if a dog wasn't disciplined, how a wild dog wasn't really free but was a prisoner. He showed me how trees and plants all had a place in nature. Suddenly I saw that if I was too wild I would miss the place that was meant for me. I understood that I could only be free if God was in charge. I saw that God had a place for me, just as he does for every plant. Mr Williams taught me that I had to find God if I was ever to find myself. I can't describe it, but it was as though some spiritual truth got through and straightened me out.'

I didn't say anything. I didn't have to. I was enjoying with Dylan a sense of friendship based on common beliefs and attitudes. He spoke again.

'In some ways, you and Mr Williams are similar. But there is a difference. He never over-stretches himself. He doesn't go looking for trouble. He seems to deal with one person at a time. But you – apart from the club, you've already got Lionel, Webster and Blondie on your back. And now you're going to add Phil Peters.'

I sighed. 'My trouble is I can't say no.' I would have sighed even deeper if I could have foreseen that within the next few months Flo Scott and Lorna Thomas would be added to that list.

Spring turned into Summer. With it came a letter from the council. In official language, it pointed out that I was failing to keep one of the terms of my tenancy. I was not maintaining the garden in good order. The accusation was true. Since moving in, I had not touched the garden. Consequently, grass was up to my knees and weeds had spread to cover the path. It was not that I was lazy, I had been too busy. It was ironic. Bet and I had spent a couple of days trimming the hedge and digging the garden for old Mr Blenkinsop. Now we were being reprimanded for not doing our own!

So one Saturday morning, we rose early and attacked the grass. Before long a number of youngsters offered their aid.

'Aid' was not quite the right word to describe Drew Sprite's efforts. He wielded the shears as a lethal weapon. After he had lopped off part of Ishbael Scott's pigtail, I took them from him. Drew became abusive, threatened me and eventually stormed off, shouting that he would break every window in my house. Although I had heard of Drew's tempers, this was my first encounter with one.

Once he had departed, the other youngsters – Ishbael and Mac Scott, Webster, Jardine, Fangs and Don – set to work with a will. By midday, the grass was low, the weeds pulled and the hedge cut. Mac was worried that Ishbael would be in trouble because of her pigtail, so I agreed to go ahead of them in order to explain to their mum.

The Scotts door was opened by a slim, dark-haired, young woman.

'Is your mum in?' I asked.

She looked at me suspiciously and eventually replied, 'My mum died years ago.'

It dawned on me that I was talking to Ishbael and Mac's mum. I had taken her for another daughter. Flo Scott had a teenage girl, Fiona, in addition to the other two, yet she still looked as young as a teenager herself. With dark eyes to match her hair, a clear complexion, a trim figure, she certainly did not give the appearance of having borne three children. Fortunately, when she realized my mistake, she was flattered and invited me in.

Although sparsely furnished, the living-room was extremely tidy. Ornaments on the mantlepiece were dusted and in line. The lino looked as though it was scrubbed every day. There was no sign of newspapers, books or toys. Mrs Scott's own appearance likewise was neat, clean and well-washed. By this time, Scott and Ishbael had arrived. I noticed that they removed their shoes before coming in.

I explained about the pigtail. Mrs Flo Scott frowned and was obviously displeased.

'Mac, why weren't you looking after your sister?'

'I'm sorry, mum,' answered the worried Mac, 'I couldn't do anything. You know what Drew's like.'

'Yes, I know what you two are like. I've told you not to play with Drew Sprite. You've disobeyed me again. I think you both deserve some punishment.'

Flo Scott went over to a drawer and took out a short cane. Mac and Ishbael fell silent. For all her girlish appearance, Mrs Scott obviously ruled her children with a rod of iron. I continued to intercede for them, pointing out that Mac and Ishbael were in no way to blame for the incident. On the contrary, they had been extremely helpful. Flo Scott relaxed, put the cane away and told the children to get on with their jobs. A relieved Mac and Ishbael disappeared into the kitchen.

'I was brought up strict myself and I want my children to respect me. I don't like the way parents round here let children do what they like, roaming the streets at all hours. I suppose that's why I don't mix much.'

Flo Scott's words confirmed what I had heard about her. She was considered a bit stand-offish by other residents. She was known to be devoted to her home but uninterested in

44

anything else. Yet for all her seeming independence, as we talked, it became clear that she was a lonely, isolated person who had faced and was facing a number of difficulties.

Perhaps it was the social worker in me, perhaps it was a warmth which developed between us, but the woman with a reputation for not communicating with neighbours began to tell me her life story.

Her father had left home when she was seven. Brought up strictly, even repressively, in a large family, she had escaped at the first opportunity. Pregnant by a soldier, she married him at the age of sixteen. Fiona was the first child and Mac followed after three years. A year later, the marriage broke up. For a while, Flo struggled in poverty to bring up her two children. Then she met and lived with Joe Scott and subsequently married him when Ishbael was conceived. Flo had never told Fiona and Mac about her first husband and they believed that Joe was their dad. She thought that Joe had less love and time for them than for Ishbael and she wanted to tell them the truth but could never pluck up courage.

The marriage to Joe had been a tempestuous one with strong disagreements over money and the amount of time he spent in the pub. Flo and Joe each appeared very suspicious about the other's fidelity. Now Joe, had departed to the seaside, as usual, to spend the summer working at a fair. He rarely wrote and sent little money. Flo was desperate to know if her husband was coming back. Financially, she was coping with the help of the Family Allowance and what little Joe did send. When she approached social security for aid, she had been told that her husband had to accept responsibility for supporting her and the children. Her anxieties were making her increasingly irritable with the children.

At this point she began to weep. Beside the strict mother and competent housewife, was a woman unsure about her capacity to keep a husband and a mum worried sick about providing for her kids on a low income. I said little except that it was marvellous how she managed to look after her children and home so well.

The following day, Ishbael knocked on our door and asked

45

if I would go round. Flo Scott's electric iron had broken down. Usually I find it difficult even to change a light bulb, but the fault was just a loose connection in the plug so I was able to mend it. Flo appeared impressed with my talents and a pattern was established. One of the children would ask me to visit and I would then help Flo with tasks ranging from fixing a washer to mending a bike.

One day, I found her sitting with her head in her hands. Tears welled in her eyes. I put a hand on her shoulder.

'Flo, what's wrong? Why the tears?'

'It's Joe. He still hasn't written. I wrote like you suggested. I know he's shacked up with some other woman. What's wrong with me? Why can't I keep a bloke?'

I tried to comfort Flo as I had on previous occasions. Her distress, though, was more severe than before. She even spoke about abandoning the children and running away. She was fed up with Edgely, disliked the neighbours, was exhausted by the children, lonely without a man and, in short, didn't care if she lived or died.

Ishbael, hearing her sobs, poked her head around the door to see what was wrong. Flo savagely told her to get out. Her reaction was so uncharacteristic that I decided some positive action was needed.

'Flo, why don't you go and see Joe? At least you could satisfy yourself about his feelings.'

'It would cost pounds to get there. And what about the kids?' Flo objected.

'I'll take you in the car,' I countered. 'The children can come too. They'd love a day out and the chance to see dad again.'

Flo brightened considerably, 'Oh thanks, Bob. I'll write today and tell him to meet us. A day out, too. I haven't been to town for a year, let alone to the seaside.'

Flo's remark reflected the restricted experiences of many folk in Edgely. There is a popular misconception that working-class people park their Jags outside council houses and holiday in Majorca. Perhaps a few do but a large number possess no car and enjoy no holidays. Flo Scott had never been to London, rarely went to large shops, and could not remember when she last had a holiday. Consequently, the combined prospect of seeing Joe and having an outing produced a state of excitement in the Scott family.

We left at 9 a.m. with Flo and Ishbael in the front seat and Fiona and Mac stretched out in the back of the mini. By five past nine we were back in the house. Ishbael had thrown up and Mrs Scott insisted on changing all her clothes. Poor Ishbael. The excitement, the car journey, the threat of a caning if she dirtied herself, was enough to make a member of the SAS feel sick. Amazingly, the white-faced Ishbael kept it down.

We arrived at Salton-on-Sea at midday. Flo was becoming increasingly tense. She began to doubt whether she should have come. She was convinced that Joe would not turn up. But, as we drove to the edge of the town, there he stood, leaning against the fence outside the fun-fair.

Joe Scott was short, thickset and possessed greasy hair swept back in what was once the Teddy Boy style. He displayed a casual manner which, so Flo informed me, women found attractive. He kissed Ishbael, nodded at Flo, ignored Mac and Fiona, and glared at me. Flo hastily introduced me as her 'social worker' and started calling me Mr Laken in such a way as to allay any suspicions that I might be her fancy man.

After a few moments staring at the pavement, I suggested we had lunch. Joe recommended a fish and chip shop. I took the three children to eat our chips on the beach, leaving Flo and Joe in the shop. After an hour, they rejoined us. Flo's arm was now through Joe's. After a few minutes sitting in the sun, Joe took Ishbael off for an icecream.

'That's right, leave us here. Ishbael's always his favourite,' complained Mac, once Mr Scott was out of sight.

'Don't be silly, of course the youngest gets more attention,' snapped Flo.

As the day progressed, we went round the arcades and the shops. Joe kept us away from the fair. He hardly spoke a word to Mac and Fiona. I could see that Flo was hurt by this but she would not say anything to offend her husband. I tried to compensate by giving my company to the two

47

children, yet felt I was helping to drive a wedge between them and Joe. At tea-time, Joe took his wife off to see the caravan where he was sleeping. I bought tea and cakes for the children. We then returned home.

On the way back, Flo expressed herself satisfied. She told me that Joe still loved her, had given her some money and had promised to come home after the season.

During the next six weeks, I took Flo down two more times to see Joe. She decided just to take Ishbael, while neighbours agreed to keep an eye on Mac and Fiona. Flo now seemed happier and I attributed the change to a greater feeling of security about her husband. But when I offered to drive her down once more, she became oddly evasive. It seemed that, having satisfied herself Joe still wanted her, she now wanted to keep him guessing. She began to wear more make-up and enjoyed a few wolf whistles in the street.

At the same time, she was becoming more dependent on me. Almost daily, Ishbael or Mac would arrive with a note requesting me to call. Then Flo would ask me to do a small repair, look at the children's homework or seek my advice on disciplining them. Meanwhile, I was trying to spend more time with Mac and Fiona, sensing that at some stage I might be needed to help them with their relationship with the man they thought was their dad.

In July, some of the youth club members suggested we went on holiday together. Trouble was, I couldn't find anywhere to go. We had no tents, so camping was out of the question. Chalets and caravans were either too expensive or already booked. Finally, I discovered that a holiday at Butlin's was cheap in late September. The date had the added attraction for some reluctant pupils that it was in school time. Accordingly, I secured twenty places and began to collect names and deposits.

One morning, Lorna Thomas stopped me in the street and, in her soft voice, politely asked if I would visit her mother to see if she could go on the holiday. Lorna was not a regular member of the club. When she came, she tended to sit on the edge of activities and wait for people to approach her. Usually, the approach did not take long. A boy would soon be trying to chat her up. Fourteen years old, with short fair hair, a turned-up nose, large lips and eyes which spoke more than her tongue, Lorna was an attractive, almost mysterious figure. I heard from others that she had few friends amongst the girls and was a poor attender at school.

The same afternoon, I called at her home. I knew that Mrs Thomas had one other child – thirteen-year-old Jules – and lived with a co-habitee named Bernard. My knock received no response. I banged again, for Lorna had said mum would be in. A sleepy voice invited me to enter. I followed the source of the voice into the living-room. It was certainly different from other rooms I had visited on the estate. Instead of a door, I had to push through rows of beads. Oil lamps and baskets of plants hung from the ceiling. The curtains were drawn and there was a kind of general haze. My eyes were drawn to a portrait of a nude woman painted in bright, jazzy colours.

'It's me. Self-portrait. Fifteen years ago.'

The voice came from the couch. Mrs Becky Thomas was still in her nightie. I guessed she'd been stoned. She was slightly built, with long blonde hair trailing across a drained, pinched face. She was not immediately recognizable as the woman in the portrait. My eyes were drawn back to it and I perceived the turned-up nose and sloe eyes which confirmed, not only the likeness, but also that she was Lorna's mum. Mrs Thomas lit a fag, sat up and spluttered.

'I'm not worth painting now. Too many fags. Too many men.'

'It's a very unusual painting, Mrs Thomas, very compelling,' I murmured, not being accustomed to discussing the merits of nude self-portraits. 'I see you read a lot as well.' The room possessed more bookshelves than wallpaper.

'Yes, astronomy, the occult, the history of art, philosophy. Not many people to talk with around here. They're just interested in football, racing and bingo. Did you know that the so-called classicial Greek democracy depended on slave labour, or that the respected Plato wanted an elitist master race?'

'Yes,' I answered, 'I had to read Plato's *Republic* when I was at college.'

Delighted to have an audience, Mrs Thomas expounded her theory that the Greek amphitheatre was connected with Stonehenge and that the Druids were the master race envisaged by Plato. Unfortunately, the writings of the Druids had been lost. However, her psychic communion with the stars had convinced her that the writings still existed and were probably buried in the hills around Edgely.

I found some difficulty in following the drift of her lecture and was relieved when she stopped in mid-sentence and asked, 'Who are you, anyway?'

I hastened to introduce myself and explained that Lorna had wanted me to call to discuss the forthcoming holiday.

'Oh yes. I wanted to make sure it was all above board. There are some strange people about these days.'

I agreed with the last remark and left with a deposit for the holiday and an invitation to call again.

The Butlin's holiday was a mixture of disaster and fun. I hired an old minibus and Dylan borrowed his dad's car. We were housed in four chalets. I stayed with Webster, Don, Jardine and Fangs. Dylan looked after Syd, Drew, Legs and Mac. Doreen Willis (along with Rebecca) shared with Lorna, Fiona, Maureen and Mo. Bet could not come because of school, which meant that the fourth chalet consisted of Gail, Ruby and Lesley Curtis on their own. Herein lay the source of some trouble.

The older boys tended to stay late in the Curtis chalet and play cards and fool about with the Curtis girls. Their antics worried me, not least because I had promised Mrs Curtis that I would keep a close eye on her daughters. Matters came to a head when other holiday-makers complained about the noise and the management threatened to send us packing. I took the chance to call our party together and, in a sensible discussion, we drew up some rules about bedtimes and behaviour.

Thereafter only two other incidents of note occurred. Ruby developed a crush on Syd and when he rejected her romantic advances – or as he put it, 'Get stuffed, you old bag' – she declared her intention of drowning herself. Strolling along the beach, she suddenly broke free from our group and rushed fully clothed into the sea. Dylan and I gave chase but need not have worried. Once the sea reached her waist, she turned round and hastily retreated to the beach.

'Grief, it's cold,' she screamed, 'I'm not going to freeze just because of that pig.' Thereafter her ardour was cooled.

The other incident was more serious. Dylan had acted as club banker. The members deposited their money with him and he distributed it each morning. The idea was a sensible one, for some would have blown the whole lot on the machines in one fling.

On the Thursday, a white-faced Dylan reported to me that money was missing from the suitcase where he kept the cash. We all met together and suspicion fell on Webster who had been seen in Dylan's chalet. He vehemently denied it.

'So what. We're all in each other's rooms. I just went to see if Legs was going swimming.'

Tension reached boiling point. Syd and Webster came to blows. I stopped them and adjourned the meeting. I spoke to Webster on his own. He continued to deny the charge and was angry that suspicion should always fall on him. When we assembled again I expressed my disappointment but said that this time I'd replace the money from project funds. In future, we determined to lodge the cash in the camp safe.

These traumas apart, the holiday was a success. A sense of group loyalty began to grow. Further, it gave me the opportunity to know the youngsters more deeply. This particularly applied to Lorna Thomas who tended to stay close to Dylan, Doreen and myself. She was careful about her appearance and discussed her make-up and clothes with Doreen. At the swimming-pool, she was adorned in the briefest of bikinis which rarely got wet. She preferred to sit on the side, enjoying the lecherous glances she received from young and old. Yet, when any males did approach her, she adopted a cool, off-hand manner.

Despite the coolness, I felt that there was a volcano

smouldering within. Certainly, she was all mixed up about her mother. She was intensely loyal to mum yet laughingly resented her weird ways. She made few comments about the co-habitee, Bernard, whom she dismissed as just another visitor who would soon disappear, only to be replaced by another. Obviously, she had never experienced a stable father figure. Perhaps this explained why she spent much of the time sitting in a café with me and talking about herself.

The week completed, we packed our gear and left. Ruby's affections had now switched to Legs Lancing. His romantic attachment was in another direction, so Ruby became more and more sullen. Nothing would please her. She complained about my driving, wanted to be in a better seat, was hungry, then thirsty. We stopped at a motorway café and at the time to leave Ruby could not be found. Eventually she was discovered in a corner wrapped around a hefty lorry driver. She refused the entreaties of her friends, declaring that she fancied the driver and was getting a lift in his lorry. The driver said nothing but it was clear from the muscular arms he was running up and down Ruby's body that an army would be required to overcome him.

There was only one ploy to use – officialdom. I produced an official-looking card (in truth it was my outdated membership of the Camping and Caravaning Club), waved it under his nose and stated, 'This girl is a ward of court. She is also under the age of sixteen. By touching her you are breaking the law in two serious respects. Please give me your name and address.'

The driver froze. Then he put Ruby down, muttered an apology and left. Ruby, astonished at my authority, meekly followed me back to the minibus.

The rest of the trip was less dramatic but more nauseating. After two motorway cafés and one hot dog van, stomachs were full. At the request of the youngsters, we stopped a couple more times for the loos. Drew Sprite asked me to stop yet again. He stepped outside, puked in a field, stepped back inside and recommenced stuffing himself with popcorn. Lorna said nothing. She was sitting at the back of the minibus where, as I occasionally observed in the mirror, she appeared to be turning green. I inquired if she was all right. She nodded. She did not get out at the stops.

We were on a dual carriageway, touching 60 m.p.h. when she suddenly slid open the window, poked out her head, and opened her mouth. The sick flew out of her mouth all right. Unfortunately, at the speed we were travelling, it flew back in and – amazingly – covered all the windows. I braked hard. For a few moments nobody spoke. I was imagining what I would have said to the police had we crashed.

'You see, officer, my front vision was completely obscured by a girl being sick at the back.'

'O yes, sir. You expect me to believe that. What you might call a sick joke.'

I was brought back to reality by the stench of Lorna's sick, the complaints of those who had received direct hits and the weeping apologies of Lorna. We had to take out all the cases and sponge down the inside of the minibus. By the time we were on our way again, the youngsters were treating it as a joke. They were concerned about Lorna and let her sit in the front, next to me. For all their roughness and occasional crudeness, some had hearts of gold. I felt warmed by the cheerfulness of their friendship.

When we finally reached home, they departed in high spirits. Lorna was the last to go. She leaned over and pecked me on the cheek.

'Thanks, Bob. That's the first holiday I've ever had.'

The weeks following the Butlin's holiday were something of an anti-climax. The youth club seemed a shade dull after our antics at camp. September gave way to October and we fell into the habit of playing football on a Saturday afternoon. Edgely possessed no pitch, so I drove the lads in relays to the nearest park. Afterwards we returned to our house to listen to the football league results over a cup of tea.

A seventeen-year-old named Stirling Drift began to play. Tall and handsome, Bet said he was a hangover from the Teddy Boy era. His black hair was heavily greased and worn with long side-burns. He was loud-mouthed and uncouth, and I did not take to him. But Bet said he had that certain something which sent shivers up girls' spines.

She was right. Ruby, who could have won a Mastermind competition on the subject of local romances, informed me that Stirling was going out with Lorna Thomas, that she was crazy about him, and that Stirling was about as faithful as Bluebeard. Having analysed Stirling's character, Ruby then had no qualms about flirting with him herself.

The mention of Lorna reminded me that I had not seen her since the holiday. She had not been to the club, I had not bumped into her in the street. I felt uneasy about her absence and her relationship with Stirling. Later that evening I asked Bet what she felt about it. She laughed.

'I think you're a bit envious, Bob. Lorna only has to bat her long eyelashes and you become all protective towards her. She's spending her time with Stirling and probably does not need anyone else.'

I grunted agreement but wasn't convinced. The following Monday I called to see Lorna. Mrs Thomas was out and Lorna had just returned from school. She greeted me cheerfully.

' 'Lo, Bob. Long time no see. Come in and have a cuppa. Sorry I haven't been to the club of late. I've got other interests now.'

Over tea, she chatted away. She was full of her friendship with Stirling. He had a motor bike and she described their rides together. She laughingly told me of the rows they had and how they enjoyed making up afterwards. Ruby was right. Lorna was crazy about him. She had seemed so reserved, so on the edge of activities, yet all the time she must have been seeking a relationship to which she could give her whole commitment. The only drawback as far as Lorna was concerned was that her mum did not approve of Stirling. Lorna dismissed this as mere jealousy because she had such a dishy bloke, while mum was stuck with 'stuffy, balding Bernard'.

I was pleased to see Lorna so happy. Her eyes were literally glowing with love. Yet some worry lurked within me. I warned her about Stirling's motor bike, for I knew that he had not passed his test and had no insurance. To be honest, though, I was worried about her emotional entanglement with Stirling. I did not want her to get hurt. I wondered how far they had gone and what the consequences might be. I could not find the words or will to express these thoughts and took my leave with the suggestion that she bring Stirling to the youth club.

Two weeks later, Lorna arrived on my doorstep at 11 p.m. Tears mixed with mascara were running down her face. She was flushed and angry.

'Lorna, what's wrong? Come in.'

'I'm not going back home, Bob. I hate my mum. She's horrible to me. Please find me somewhere else to live.'

We took her in and fed her tea and toast. Bet sat beside her. At first, Lorna insisted that her mum was jealous and wanted her to stop seeing Stirling. Then she said more.

'It's not just that. She caught us tonight. Mum and Bernard went to the films but came back early. And . . . well . . . I was in bed with Stirling. I don't care. I love him. I want to make love with him. She slung him out and told him not to come back. She called me a dirty bitch. She said that if I did it with the likes of Stirling I'd do it with anyone. I wouldn't mind, but look at the blokes she's had. I don't even know who my dad is. I told her that and I said that at least I wasn't having it off with Bernard. She told me to clear out.'

Lorna stopped and buried her face in Bet's shoulder. Bet just patted her as she sobbed.

'Lorna, of course you can stay here,' I assured her, 'providing that your mum agrees. She does care about you. She wouldn't have carried on so if she didn't worry about you. I know it seems inconsistent but perhaps she wants you to avoid some of the mistakes she made. I must go and see her.'

Mrs Becky Thomas did not seem surprised to see me. She probably anticipated that her daughter would run to our house. She was still fuming.

'I know what you're thinking, Bob. Who am I to tell my daughter what to do. Well, I learnt the hard way. I got into trouble by falling for blokes just like Stirling Drift. He's no good for her. He's just using her for a few cheap thrills. He'll never get a regular job and make her a home. He's just a layabout. I want Lorna to have a better life than I've had.'

Meanwhile, Bernard sat and watched TV. He seemed uninterested in Becky, Lorna or me.

'Yes, I do want her back,' Mrs Thomas went on. 'But she's got to change. She's got to listen to me.'

Mrs Thomas accompanied me back to our home. Mother and daughter then sat and talked for an hour. Lorna promised to be careful with Stirling and Becky promised to try to like him. I was amazed at Mrs Thomas. She was calm and in control of herself. She was so unlike the dozy, stoned woman I'd met the first time. Perhaps, I mused to myself, these changes of moods created problems for Lorna. She could never be sure how her mum would react. They did not leave until 1 a.m. Another late night. But keeping them together was worth some lost sleep.

If I thought the Thomas affair was over, I could not have been more wrong. During the next month, Lorna popped in to see me a few times for a chat and gave the impression that all was going well. She did not bring Stirling but did persuade him to attend the youth club. When I tried to talk to him about Lorna, he was evasive and uncomfortable. He laughingly tried to create the impression that his romance with Lorna was not to be taken seriously.

I visited Mrs Thomas once more. On this occasion, she had reverted back to her hazy, astrologist role. Draped in a long garment which stretched to the floor, she was smoking heavily and drinking what I took to be brandy. She brushed aside my queries about Lorna, asked my date of birth and began to explain the connection between my character and the stars. I left feeling that there were two Mrs Thomases.

A few evenings later, Jules Thomas knocked with a note from mum asking me to come 'urgently'. When I arrived, Mrs Thomas was slumped in a chair with a face to match the black sweater she was wearing. Lorna was sniffing, trying hard to hold back tears.

'Here's Bob,' Becky Thomas snorted. 'Now tell him what you told me.'

Lorna looked out of the window and whispered, 'I'm pregnant.'

'Pregnant? How can you be?' I asked. It was a ridiculous question but I was thinking that she and Stirling had only been going out together for a few weeks.

'I've been going with Stirling for months,' Lorna said. 'He wanted to keep it secret until recently. Don't worry, he loves me. And I'm glad.' She ended her statement on a defiant note.

'Well, I'm not,' Mrs Thomas cut in. 'You don't know what you're doing. I had you when I was young. It spoils your childhood. You're still a schoolgirl. Bob, tell her she can have an abortion.'

I was not prepared to persuade Lorna to abort. If necessary, I would inform her of the options which were open to her. But first I wanted to establish the facts. Apparently Lorna had announced her pregnancy because her period was well overdue. Mrs Thomas had accepted her announcement, welcomed it by belting Lorna around the face and promptly sent for me. I suggested she saw Dr Keen. I rang our friendly GP at his home and he suggested that we bring in a specimen of Lorna's urine.

At this point the medical procedures met an unusual hitch. The following morning, Lorna presented me with a specimen in an old wine bottle. Lionel had dropped in for a cup of tea which I sent him to make while I was on the phone. I was disturbed by a spluttering sound and rushed in to find Lionel clutching his throat. The old rogue had helped himself to a crafty swig of the wine bottle.

'Oh Bob, I just fancied a tiny drop. What wine is it? It's awful. It tastes just like . . .'

Almost collapsing with laughter, I told Lionel that his taste buds were correct. Lionel could keep most things down, but on hearing the news, he made a dash for the loo, to emerge later as a paler, wiser old man.

A week after this, Becky, Lorna and I attended the surgery to hear the test results. Dr Keen confirmed that Lorna was pregnant. He spoke gently to her, explaining that she would have to decide whether to apply for an abortion, to place the child for adoption, or to keep the baby. Lorna promptly replied that she was going to keep it. Mrs Thomas asked how she could possibly do that while she was still at school. Who would pay? Who would look after it? Ron Keen cut her short and said Lorna must have time to think.

'Of course, there is another person involved,' our young GP continued, 'and he's not even here today.' He was referring to Stirling. On hearing about the possible pregnancy, Stirling had started to avoid Lorna. He sent feeble excuses like, 'Having my hair cut' or 'Have to sign on for the dole'. Amazingly, Lorna accepted them and remained convinced that he would stand by her. Sensing Stirling's attitude, Dr Keen became more blunt.

'Bob, no doubt you will be seeing this Stirling. You might point out to him that he could find himself in court for having sex with a young girl. He will also have financial obligations.' Turning to Lorna, he added, 'But don't worry about that. You're pregnant and you'll need good care.'

Christmas came. At Ted Williams suggestion, I had hired the church hall for an afternoon and evening a few days before Christmas Day. A group of parents were busy putting the final touches to the preparations for an afternoon party for the children. Webster, the Curtis girls, Fiona Scott and Legs Lancing were collecting records for the evening disco for the teenagers. I was perched on a tall ladder sticking some coloured paper over a bulb when the ladder legs were shaken violently. Looking down, I suppressed a groan. Lionel was there, looking very aggrieved and waving some Christmas wrapping paper.

The youth club had distributed presents to elderly people who lived alone. Mostly the presents were food but I'd ensured that Lionel was given a pair of pants. I'd been informed by his landlord that he did not use pants, so I bought him a good pair. It didn't occur to Lionel to express thanks.

'Pants, I don't want pants. I want a vest, a nice, warm vest.'

My initial reaction was to stuff the pants down his ungrateful throat. Resisting the temptation, I suggested that if he took them back the shop would probably exchange them for a vest.

'I've tried that and they refused, just because I was wearing them.'

Words failed me. I resumed my task, leaving Lionel to try to nick some of the food. The grub was being arranged by Mrs Roly Williams, Mrs Battle, Mrs Peters, Mrs Barnes and Mrs Plumb. I told Daphne Peters that I had been thinking of Phil in Borstal and had written to him. The only disappointment was that Flo Scott, who had promised to help, did not turn up. Red Curtis had generously supplied some cakes and parents contributed sandwiches.

At 2.30 p.m. we opened the doors, which were being hammered on by the kids. Including adults, over a hundred bodies were crammed into the hall. Dylan showed yet more of his abilities in the skilful way he ran the games. The mums then served tea. I had to stop Drew Sprite and Jules Thomas from throwing doughnuts at each other but otherwise all went smoothly. Afterwards, the Rev. Wantage used the church projector to show some cartoons.

Finally, Father Christmas, alias Mr Plumb, arrived. His large girth and deep voice fitted him for the part and he distributed small presents to all the children. He successfully resisted the efforts of Troy Peters to pull off his cotton wool beard and of Wally Blake to pour lemonade down his boots. He departed to three hearty cheers.

By 4.30 the party was officially over but more grown-ups drifted in. Red Curtis turned out to be a bit of a pianist and an impromptu singsong commenced, made up of a curious mixture of Christmas carols and bawdy ditties. Blondie Blake, who did not usually mix in well with the community, turned up and gave Dylan and me a kiss under the mistletoe.

I noticed Mrs Thomas standing with Bernard. Bet nudged me and pointed to the door. Lorna Thomas had arrived.

Since our visit to Dr Keen, Lorna had stuck to her decision

to have the baby. After an initial attempt to persuade her otherwise, Mrs Thomas had not only accepted the decision but now seemed to be looking forward to her first grandchild. Indeed, she indulged in complicated calculations as to what would be the best date for the birth, from the point of view of which stars would shape the newborn's personality.

Lorna's relationship with Stirling could only be described as stormy. Her apparent reserve of character, as I suspected, hid a volcano. Stirling's lack of enthusiasm for the birth, his failure to contribute one penny towards costs, her suspicions that he still went with other girls, led to noisy rows in the streets. During one, Stirling slapped Lorna around the face and she laid him low with a kick between his legs. Yet the rowdy scenes were followed by sweet reconciliations.

As Lorna walked into the hall, she looked almost angelic. Pregnancy seemed good for her health. Her fair hair was shining, her skin was fresher than ever. Her expressive lips smiled shyly as she looked around the room. Her pregnancy was now obvious to all and she made no secret of it. Somehow, the entrance of an unmarried, pregnant young girl seemed appropriate to Christmas, and my emotions were deeply touched. Here was a schoolgirl who had never known her own father. She had a strange mother and an unreliable boyfriend. Yet in her womb she carried life and, despite all the disadvantages surrounding the birth, that small life would come into the world with hope and love. It was Christmas.

4

Scott Family Saga

Early in the new year, Bet and I started going regularly to the chapel run by Ted Williams. We had attended a few services at St Matthew's, where we had been made welcome, and also been to most of the fashionable churches in the town centre. But the chapel was where we felt at home.

The inside of Ted's chapel was no more attractive than its gaunt exterior. Whitewashed walls were turning yellow with damp. The paintwork was brown and peeling. The floor consisted of bare boards or, in places, the rotting remains of bare boards. The hymn-books were so old they could have been used by John Wesley himself and the musical accompaniment came from a foot-pedal type organ which wheezed and groaned like an old steam train. Worst limitation of all the chapel possessed no running water. Worshippers in dire need of a loo had to rely on the mercy of nearby householders. Water for the after-service cup of tea had to be brought along in flasks.

Despite all these hardships, the atmosphere was not gloomy or austere. On the contrary, it was bright and cheerful. Thanks entirely to Ted Williams.

Ted was short, with shoulders like an American gangster. He was blessed with a sunny disposition which always sought to see the positive in any difficulty. So, in Ted's eyes, the chapel's lack of water was an advantage as it meant they never suffered from burst or frozen pipes. He had spent all his forty years on the Edgely estate and his ruddy complexion suggested that he was a farmer. In fact, he made his living as a self-employed window cleaner but he took every opportunity to tramp around the surrounding countryside.

He had stumbled across the chapel when cleaning some windows nearby. It had been unused for years and he

61

obtained permission from its trustees to open it again. With his own hands, he made good the roof and then opened the chapel for services which he led. He was fired by the belief that Christianity was for ordinary people like the residents of Edgely and not just for the commuters who travelled in to fashionable churches.

When Bet and I first went, there were about fifteen people in attendance. Ted's wife, Roly, and their three daughters, Miss Bird – who reminded me of an energetic sparrow – Dylan and Doreen along with their Rebecca, old Mr Blenkinsop, Mrs Barnes and her married daughter, Mrs Devlin – a woman of about thirty whom I had not met before – and her small son, and the inevitable Lionel.

The service was simple and short. Ted did not prepare anything in writing, yet it proceeded in orderly fashion. His face seemed a perpetual smile and, when the Devlin baby started yelling, he showed no annoyance but just picked him up and continued his talk.

The talks can only be described as narrative parables. Ted told them around three main themes. There were talks about his father who had been well known in the area as an open-air wrestler and strong man; talks about Ted's own childhood, when he had got into all kinds of boyish scrapes; and talks about the countryside, about trees, animals and farms. They were told with gusto and humour and then related to a story in the Bible. It became clear that the window-cleaning preacher was using updated parables to convey the truths taught by Jesus. The stories made compulsive listening and, combined with the friendliness of everyone, created an environment which Bet and I looked forward to each Sunday.

Lorna's baby was born in the Spring. She decided to have him christened in the chapel. Ted was not authorized to perform this ceremony, but he held what he called a 'thanksgiving service'. The chapel was packed, for a number of other local families joined the regular worshippers. Mrs Becky Thomas wore a long, flowing garment decorated with figures of black cats. She was accompanied by Bernard, looking uncomfortable in a black suit. Stirling Drift did not turn up, although he had promised to do so.

A woman who read the stars, her co-habitee, an unmarried mum – not the usual congregation in a church. Yet Ted was delighted. He told me afterwards that Christianity was for just these people and was not confined to the 'drivers of Rovers and Mercedes'.

The service was very simple. A few familiar hymns, a short talk consisting mainly of Ted telling hilarious stories about his own babies, and then the thanksgiving. Lorna stood up proudly clutching new-born Elvis (named, of course, after her favourite rock star). Ted then placed his huge hand on the tiny head and prayed, giving thanks to God for the young life. He then asked old Mr Blenkinsop and Mrs Barnes to hold the baby while he offered thanks for all parents and grandparents. Finally, Ted said that we all had a responsibility to help Lorna look after Elvis.

Elvis remained quiet until the last hymn. Then he began to render a noisy imitation of his more famous namesake. Following the service, we all adjourned to the Thomas's home for cakes and sandwiches. Since cash was short we toasted the baby in tea and coffee.

Several youngsters had attended the service. They were amazed that a sermon could be so lively and after that a few began to attend the chapel on Sunday evenings. Usually they would drop into our home for a cuppa before piling into the mini-van for the drive to the service. Webster was one. He usually sat at the back next to the oil stove and helped distribute the hymn-books. A collecting-box was also kept at the rear and I resolved to keep an eye on it. Mac and Ishbael Scott, Drew Sprite, Jardine and Troy Peters, Syd and Fangs Battle and the Curtis girls were also amongst the regulars. Although they all listened attentively, the youngsters also made a lot of noise.

My respect for Ted deepened as I observed the way he dealt with them. He never threatened to kick them out, yet he did not ignore the disturbances. When the girls were giggling amongst themselves during a hymn, he just approached them and grinned. The message conveyed was 'I'm on your side but please be a bit quieter'. When Mac and Ishbael started fighting, he lifted Ishbael up and continued his talk while carrying the delighted child on his shoulders.

Lesley Curtis, provoked beyond endurance by the poking and pinching from Drew, suddenly gave him a sharp backhander across the face. Drew jumped on the bench, called her a tart and belted her back. Ted's reaction was to motion to Dylan to sit between the offenders and to use the incident as an illustration in the talk he was giving about self-control. The kids laughed; the point was driven home.

After the service, we dropped into the habit of driving to the nearest fish and chip shop – on the next estate – and then chatting as we consumed our chips in the street outside. For some reason these chats became intimate, personal affairs. Perhaps it was the after-effect of Ted's sermon. Perhaps it was the cosiness of sitting on a wall under a lamp-post, where the yellow light mingled with the steam from our chips. Whatever the reason, the conversations took on a serious note.

Sometimes we discussed the meaning of Ted's talk. Obviously, some were taking him seriously. One Sunday, Ted had spoken about the stealing he did when he was a boy and likened himself to the biblical Matthew, the thieving tax collector. Fangs Battle was much impressed and admitted that he was always shoplifting but that since going to the chapel he had started to pray for strength to stop. Others began to tell tales of their nicking. Drew boasted about his break-ins to garages, claiming that he now possessed £400 worth of electrical tools.

Suddenly he turned to me. 'Will you shop us, Bob? I suppose you'll tell the pigs.'

'Or our parents,' put in Troy.

I had already considered this issue, knowing it would have to be faced.

'No, I won't shop you,' I said. 'But make no mistake, I'm not encouraging you. I think Ted has explained why nicking is wrong. I want to help you stop.'

My words seemed stilted – even pious – to me, yet they seemed to deepen the trust between us and the youngsters began to reveal more and more of their problems in these chip encounters. Then one evening, as we were about to leave I felt a hand in mine. Looking down, I saw little Ishbael Scott. I picked her up, tears were in her eyes. I asked her gently, 'What's up, Ishbael? Haven't you got any chips?'

'My mum keeps crying. You see her, Bob, please?'

I couldn't refuse such a request and the very next morning I knocked on Flo Scott's door.

'Oh, it's you, Bob.' Flo hesitated before asking me in. Flo's attitude was reserved and withdrawn, even by her standards. I had begun to take a pride in my achievement of getting her to communicate with myself and others. Now she didn't want to talk about Joe, she wasn't complaining about the behaviour of the children and she didn't have any outstanding odd jobs. The only normal thing was her obsession with housework. She was moving around the room doing the dusting – probably for the umpteenth time that day.

'What is it, Flo? You look so worried.'

In reply, Flo took a buff envelope out of a drawer and handed it to me. I drew out an official-looking notice. A summons. Flo was to appear in court accused of defrauding social security of £66. Screwing the duster in her hands, Flo told me that she had informed social security that she and Joe were legally separated and that he was not supporting her. Thus for a short period she had received money 'under false pretences'.

'I had to do it, Bob. I couldn't manage on what Joe was sending. I didn't want to ask you for money. You've done so much already.'

I felt a mixture of shame and anger. Shame that I had not perceived the extent of her financial difficulties, anger that she should be prosecuted. Flo was now sobbing.

'Bob, I'll end up in prison. The man who came here said I might. What will happen to the children? They'll be put in a Home. Don't let them go.'

To my embarrassment, Flo had fallen on her knees and was weeping against my legs. I gently lifted her up.

'No, Flo. They won't leave this house. I promise you that. Just give me the name of that official.'

In a cold fury, I phoned the social security office. I was passed from official to official, told that Mrs Scott's file had been lost and advised to phone back. I insisted, and eventually contacted the one who had visited Flo. I arranged to see him the next day.

The headquarters of social security was a huge plate glassed building situated a mile to the north of the town centre. A uniformed attendant led me through a maze of corridors where I met Mr Phelps, who had visited Flo, and Mr Green, an assistant manager. I tried to persuade them to remove the charge against Flo with the guarantee that our project would repay the money. Mr Phelp's droopy moustache began to bristle.

'Mr Laken, I am sympathetic but you social workers must realize that we are dealing with public money and that people must learn to be honest with it. Your soft approach would do no good. Mrs Scott would just take your hand-out and before long she'd be on the fiddle again. Mrs Scott is a thief. She knew the penalties and now she must take the consequences.'

The man's words and his pontificating manner irritated me. I pointed out how little income Flo was receiving, how she had struggled for so long, how honest she was in general. Mr Phelps was not impressed. He cut in, 'Do you know, Mr Laken, how little we public officials earn? Why some of these people receive more in social benefits than we do in wages. Yet we are expected to be honest all the time.'

I played my next card.

'You threatened Mrs Scott with prison and said her children would go into a Home. I believe you were very wrong to alarm her in this way. She's almost beside herself with fear. And just supposing she did go to prison. If the children were taken into care the cost to the public would be a hundred times the £66. But even that is nothing compared with the emotional harm it would do to the children if they were separated from their mother.'

My revelation that Mr Phelps had threatened Flo seemed to annoy Mr Green. He gave a sharp glance at Mr Phelps. The latter flushed and responded, ' . . . umm, I would not say I threatened Mrs Scott. I merely pointed out that one of the possible outcomes of such a case is a prison sentence. As for your plea about the children going into care, it is irrelevant. She should have thought of the consequences before stealing. Our concern is to ensure that money is not abused. You social workers must look after the children.'

Aware that I was getting nowhere fast with the obdurate Mr Phelps, I appealed to his superior.

'Mr Green, as a manager you can take decisions. You know very well that people are not always prosecuted for crimes. People who fiddle income tax to the tune of thousands are not taken to court if they return even part of the money. So why not overlook this minor case?'

The assistant manager had his stock reply. I could imagine him having learnt it at some high-level, civil service seminar.

'Ah, it's all a matter of policy, Mr Laken. It is the policy of inland revenue not to prosecute in most cases. It is the policy of this organization to prosecute in all cases. We can not make exceptions. Policy cannot be concerned with the needs of individuals. I am truly sorry for Mrs Scott but it would upset all the processes of our administration if we began to make exceptions. If you had presented today some evidence casting doubt on Mrs Scott's guilt then I might have withdrawn the prosection. But she actually admits it. There is nothing more to be said.'

At least Mr Green had been polite and I reckoned he would have words with his subordinate about his attitude to clients. But I had no comfort for Flo. On my return, I could only say that I would attend court with her and would try to speak on her behalf.

A month later, we were waiting at the Magistrates' Court. For the hundredth time, I assured Flo that the chances of a prison sentence were minimal but that, if the unexpected did occur, Bet and I would look after the children.

After an hour and a half, Flo's case was called. She looked pale and tense as she was ushered into the dock. I had already approached the clerk of the court and received permission to sit at the back, and to speak.

In my experience, magistrates in juvenile courts make great efforts to be understanding and sympathetic. The same cannot always be said for the adult bench. The chairman was Major Gowans, a former Oxford rowing blue, governor of a well-known local public school and possessor of a large unearned income. His two colleagues on the bench were Mrs Florence Digsby, wife of a local gentleman farmer, and Miss Rhona Gifford, a wealthy horse breeder. I groaned inwardly, fearing that this trio were unlikely to have had much experience of bringing up three kids on a low income on a council estate.

The clerk read out the charges. Mr Phelps, puffed up with self-importance, stood smartly to attention and recited the facts of the case. He revealed how he had suspected Mrs Scott's statements and how, under his probing, she had confessed. Flo then stood up, her eyes downward, and pleaded guilty. She had nothing to say on her own behalf and the clerk motioned me forward.

I portrayed the pressures Flo was under, the inadequate support from her husband, how she was struggling to bring up a family. I pointed out how well she was doing, that she was respected as an honest person and that the children were well-behaved members of our club. I paused. Major Gowans nodded and I sat down feeling that I needn't have bothered. The magistrates then retired.

We did not have long to wait. On their return, Flo was instructed to remain standing. Major Gowans then proceeded to deliver a lecture.

'Mrs Scott, we have considered your case. All that can be said in your favour is that you have admitted your guilt. There is far too much abuse of social security. The state is continually giving people money and it just encourages them to grab more. It is no excuse that your husband works away. You do receive Family Allowance. Other people manage without being dishonest. Our decision is that you are fined £100 and must repay the £66.'

I groaned.

Flo went white and then red – angry red. She clenched her fists and burst out, 'How can I afford another £100? I

68

haven't got any money, that's why I did this. What do you know about it? You look as though you spend more on booze then I do on my kids.'

Pointing to the fur coat worn by Mrs Digsby, she continued, 'That fur costs more than I can spend in a year and you've got the cheek to say I've got no excuse. Have you ever gone without food so you can pay the rent? Do you have to buy your clothes from jumble sales?'

By this time the three magistrates were on their feet. I jumped forward to quieten Flo. Much as I agreed with her sentiments, I knew she could be imprisoned for contempt of court. Breathing heavily, controlling himself with difficulty, Major Gowans ordered her out, telling her she was lucky not to be on the way to the cells.

Once outside the courtroom, Flo began to shake violently. She wept all over me. Over a cup of coffee, I told Flo that the project was prepared to repay the £66 but that she would still have to pay off the fine at two pounds a week. Despite her current lack of enthusiasm for Joe, she determined to write to him and to ask for regular payments – or else. Finally, she did raise a grin.

'Cor, Bob, I told that red-nosed git a thing or two. Just because they got posh names and voices, they think they can treat us like dirt. I bet I work harder than those three put together.'

We drove home. Flo was so relieved that the ordeal was over and that she had not lost her freedom, she seemed almost exhilarated. Her feeling did not last long. That evening the local paper reported the case. Under the heading 'Magistrate Slams Sponger', details were given of Flo's name, address and offence. Knowing what had happened, other children in the street began to taunt Fiona, Mac and Ishbael.

'What's your mum been up to, then?'

'Thought you Scotts were all respectable and didn't mix with the likes of us.'

'Your mum shouldn't be so stuck up. She's just like the rest of us.'

Flo was deeply humiliated. She withdrew into herself and would not venture outside for days. I called in regularly and tried to cheer her up. As she sat brooding, feeling sorry for herself, I could hardly believe this was the same person who had stood up in that courtroom, fist waving in the air, while she gave the magistrates a piece of her mind.

As Flo retreated into her home once more, so she returned to the pattern of dependence upon me. I continued to call regularly and voiced my concern about the Scott family's relationship with Joe. Eventually, I suggested to Flo that I took her and the children to see him again. Flo looked up from pouring a cup of tea.

'It's over with Joe. He never even bothered to reply after that court case. Just sent me £10, and that doesn't go far. I've written again to tell him never to come back. Bob, I want you to help me get a proper legal separation, then I will be able to draw the social security money.'

I wasn't surprised. Joe had come home for a couple of weeks at Christmas and then returned to the seaside, saying he had a permanent job in one of the arcades. Thereafter the money he sent to Flo was intermittent to say the least. No doubt financially she would be better off to be officially separated from him. Nonetheless, the break-up of a marriage has emotional implications for all the participants.

Flo continued, 'I'm pretty sure he's got a tart down there. He's never gone back there after Christmas in other years.'

'But what about the children? What effect will this have on them?' I protested, amazed at the cool, detached manner with which Flo was conducting the demise of her marriage.

'What about them?' she countered. 'They don't miss him. You saw how he treated Mac and Fiona. It was just the same at Christmas. Expensive presents for Ishbael and plastic muck for Fiona and Mac. Anyway, he's not their dad. And don't tell me that Ishbael misses him. She never mentions his name.'

Still I persisted. 'Flo, you were so eager to see him last summer. And you seemed happy together. You did miss him.'

'Yes, I did. But what did he want from me? While you were left looking after the children on the beach, he took me back to his caravan. OK, he's good in bed and I need that. But I want more. I want a bloke who cares for me, who is a real person. And I'll tell you something else, I'm fed up with being trodden on. Remember how I stood up to that magistrate snob in court? That did me good. I enjoyed it. I'm going to make decisions for myself. I'm working out what I want from life and I'm not letting Joe Scott use me as a doormat.'

The experience in court and her reflections about marriage had prompted Flo to think seriously about life. She was going through a period of discovery and self-assessment. She wanted to talk about religion, politics, the community. She probed for my views on social work and education. Although unread and almost untaught, she revealed an inquiring mind. It excited me to see her mind blossoming, though I sometimes worried about the direction it would take. I suppose she wanted to work out a philosophy for her life.

As she explained, 'Until recently I've never really thought about what I've been doing. Take my caning the children. I do it because I feel it is right. I know you disagree and you can give reasons for your views. You and Bet seem to be able to put feelings together with thinking and then into words. You've been doing it for years. I'm just starting.'

As well as thinking and talking, Flo had begun to live differently. She had a younger sister in a nearby town with whom she had almost lost touch. In the past, I had heard Flo speak disapprovingly of Val, who was a divorcee and a bit of a man-chaser. Now Flo deliberately sought Val out and began going to discos with her. While she was away, Fiona was left to look after Mac and Ishbael. Sometimes Flo would return in the early hours of the morning. No wonder the neighbours started gossiping. Flo, from being almost a recluse was now becoming a night bird.

Then a few weeks later, Flo announced to me, 'Bob, I've found it. The real thing. Love. His name is Ritchie. I want him to come and live here. But I want your advice first.'

Flo's words sent alarm bells ringing in my head. What would be the effect on the children? What about Joe? How would the neighbours react? What was Ritchie like?

71

I soon found out about Ritchie Crosby, whom Flo had met at a disco. He was separated from his wife but had no children. He had a reputation as a heavy drinker. At least he had a trade and was in employment as a roofer. Flo brought him round to meet me. He was blond, tall and sharp-featured. In contrast to Joe, he was articulate and had obviously charmed Flo off her feet. He came straight to the point.

'You probably think I'm after Flo for one thing and once I've got it I'll leave her. No way. I've really fallen for her. I want to be with her all the time.'

As he spoke, Flo looked adoringly into his eyes and intertwined her fingers with his. She listened as I spoke.

'What about Fiona, Mac and Ishbael? How will they cope with losing Joe and a new man moving in?'

'Come off it, Bob,' Flo countered. 'You know that Joe always ignored Fiona and Mac. And Ishbael hardly ever mentions him.' She was trying to reason her fears away. I was still not convinced.

'Children are not china ornaments who can be moved from owner to owner without feeling any effect. Fiona and Mac still don't know the truth about their real dad. Nothing I say will change your feelings but I do advise you to go slowly, so that you don't make a wrong decision. And if Ritchie does move in, give the children time to adapt.'

'I suppose you think marriage is sacred,' Flo retorted with some spirit, and that I should stick to Joe no matter how badly he treats me. Does a lousy marriage have to come before the happiness of individuals? I want a man who is here. I want sex. I want love. What about *me*?'

Ritchie cut in. 'And I want happiness. I know I can be happy with Flo. We're just made for each other. Don't persuade Flo to turn against me, Bob, she takes notice of what you say.'

'Yes, I do believe in marriage,' I said. 'I believe God wants people to stay with each other. I believe that children turn out best when they've got two parents who love each other and stick together. But I know how unhappy Flo has been and I realize she's got to find fulfilment in her own life. All

I'm asking is that you take time before committing yourselves to each other, that you consider what it will mean for the children, and that you remember you each already have a partner.'

As a result of our talk, they agreed to wait before making any decisions. Just one week later Ritchie moved in. I watched what followed with interest and concern. Initially, at least, Mac and Ishbael accepted the changes very calmly. Ritchie made great efforts to be like a father. He was adept at sport and often kicked a ball around with Mac in the back yard. The fact that he was in work meant that the family's financial hardships eased.

However, if the younger children accepted Ritchie, the neighbours did not. Extramarital affairs were not uncommon in the locality but Flo was condemned for bringing in another man while her husband was away. They knew nothing about Flo's previous decision to finish with Joe and considered that she and Ritchie were having a fling while Joe was working hard to support her. Mrs Battle's tongue was especially venomous.

'The cheap tart,' she spat out. 'She's too good to mix with us yet as soon as her bloke's back is turned she lets someone else get in the bed.'

Flo had never mixed much with the neighbours and was quite prepared to ignore the comments. Ritchie, though, found it galling to be 'sent to Coventry' as soon as he arrived.

Even more serious was the effect of the changes on Fiona. Normally quiet, reticent and self-effacing, it might have been anticipated that she of all the family would have taken things in her stride. On the contrary. She had recently started going out with Legs Lancing and it was well known that Fiona would not let him go too far with her. I admired her controlled, responsible behaviour.

Now, with the arrival of Ritchie, she seemed to be saying, 'If my mum can sleep around, why should I restrain myself?' Fiona took to wearing make-up and low-cut blouses and allowed the delighted Legs to become much more familiar.

Flo was very upset. She had ruled the children with a rod of iron, and told her daughter she was still not too old for a good hiding. Fiona's spirited response took her completely aback.

'All right. Do you want me to take my pants down? Your fancy man might like that. He's not too fussy who he touches.'

The other major difficulty provoked by Ritchie's arrival was what to do about Joe. To her credit, Flo refused to handle it by sending a letter to her husband. She insisted on tackling Joe face to face with the news that someone else had moved it. She declined Ritchie's offer to accompany her on the mission.

Accordingly, one summer's morning I found myself driving Flo and Ishbael to Joe's seaside residence. It was very different from a few months earlier, when we had made the same journey because Flo wanted him to come home. This time she had written, arranging to meet him on an 'urgent matter'. As usual, he had not replied but as I parked the van I saw him waiting at the table in the café.

I bought teas for us all. I had suggested to Flo that I should withdraw with Ishbael in order to let them pursue their confidential talk. Disconcertingly, Flo pleaded with me to stay throughout the interview in case Joe became violent. Such faith in my prowess at martial arts was touching but I didn't fancy my chances against the thickset Joe. Perhaps Flo reckoned she could escape while I was being battered to pulp! Anyway, I stayed. I listened to Flo floundering around as she sought to raise the subject. Ishbael was sitting on Joe's knee. She had no problem in focussing attention on the 'urgent matter'.

'Daddy,' she said, 'Uncle Ritchie is sleeping in your bed.'

Joe turned pale, then red. Beads of sweat glistened on his face as he sought to control his temper. A plastic spoon snapped between his fingers. Flo drew several deep breaths.

'That's why I've come to see you. I told you before that it was all over between us. That had nothing to do with any other blokes. Well, now I have met someone else and he's living with me. I'm in love with him. I want to marry him.'

Flo was white, tense and brave. She answered truthfully

the barrage of questions that Joe blasted at her. She told him about Ritchie, how she met him, how many times she had slept with him. Joe raged bitterly, not seeming to care that his loud voice was being eagerly listened to by the other customers in the crowded café. He accused Flo of being a slut, a bad mother and the laughing-stock of the street. He was bitter about this other man, who was ruining his marriage and stealing his children from him.

A middle-aged couple left their table and, as the woman passed, she glared at me. It was my turn to redden as I realized that, sitting between Flo and Joe and now looking after Ishbael, I had all the appearance of the guilty third party.

However, as far as Flo and Joe were concerned, I might as well have been invisible for all the notice they took of me. After suffering Joe's insults for several minutes, Flo hit back. He was not exactly a model of pure morality himself. He had hardly discharged his duties as a father and was never seen in the street.

'All right,' confessed Joe. 'I don't deny I've been with other women down here. But they've meant nothing to me. I've always loved you and you alone.'

He leant over the table and grasped Flo's arm, twisting it until the pain showed in her face. She made no effort to restrain him.

'I'm coming back,' Joe hissed. 'It's my home. They're my children. You're my woman. I'll work out my notice and then I'll return. If this Ritchie nut is still in the house, I'll break his back.'

Joe then stormed out of the café.

Once he had disappeared, I expected Flo to be full of hate towards him. To my surprise, she rolled up her sleeve and showed me the red marks where Joe had grasped her.

'Look at that, Bob. He's not the man to lose his woman without a struggle. He really must love me.'

I groaned inwardly. I was wondering what had happened to the woman who wanted to be treated like a person, not a possession. I was imaging what would occur when Joe did return and how the children would react to the latest twist in the Scott family saga.

These dismal thoughts were interrupted by the menacing arrival of the café manager who, in not very polite language, told me that his customers were fed up with hearing about my affairs and that I should take my girl friend with me and not return.

I felt so miserable, I didn't have the heart to argue. Instead I left – with the parting shot that I would not have given him my custom if I had realized that the café was so low-class as to use plastic teaspoons!

During the following two weeks, Flo visited me frequently. She was in a state of high excitement. She had told Ritchie of Joe's threat and he promptly replied that if Joe showed his face in the house it would be smashed in. Worse, Ishbael was pleading for her dad to come back while Mac said he preferred Ritchie. Fiona threw in the bitter observation that Joe and Ritchie would probably kill each other and then her mum would be free to pick up some other bloke.

Joe did return. Neighbours were watching through the curtains. Mac had been primed by Flo to rush for me should a fight break out – although I did not fancy getting between the two combatants. In the event, the homecoming was something of an anti-climax. The two men muttered, snarled, threatened and swore at each other but were too afraid of losing face by a defeat and so made excuses not to fight.

Joe stated, quite correctly, that the rent book was still in his name and that he had every right to stay.

Ritchie pointed out, with equal validity, that Flo had invited him in, that he was paying the rent and that Flo had agreed to marry him.

A bizarre form of *menage à trois* was thus established. Flo refused to sleep with either man and moved into Fiona's bedroom. Ritchie slept in Flo's room. Joe kipped on the settee.

It became obvious that Flo was playing one man off against the other. She assured Ritchie that she loved and would marry him. Yet she did not completely reject Joe's advances and allowed him to cuddle and kiss her. She constantly sought my opinion, which was simply that she would have to make it quite clear which man she wanted to stay and which to go. The trouble was that Flo enjoyed having the two compete for her favours and she was really reluctant to bring the drama to an end. In addition, Joe and Ritchie were also calling – at different times – to see me, in order to spell out the rival's faults and win my support in ejecting him.

Declining both the frying-pan and the fire, I refused to take sides and suggested that the two men, Flo and myself, should discuss the issue in the open. Flo rejected the proposal on the grounds that the meeting would result in violence. I suspected that her real reason was her fear of having to voice a definite preference for one of the two.

Before I had time to press the suggestion with Flo, Ritchie told me of his plan. He reckoned that if Joe accepted that Flo loved him (Ritchie), he would leave. So, having told Flo that Joe had gone to town to sign on, Ritchie persuaded her to make love on the settee. Joe walked in and, in a raging temper, ordered Flo to choose between Ritchie and him. Flo opted for Ritchie. Joe then declared he would throw himself under the next express train. Flo and Ritchie began to plead with him not to kill himself.

Ritchie rushed round to me, to see if I could stop Joe 'from doing anything silly'. Oddly enough, Ritchie now seemed concerned about Joe and wanted me to persuade him to stay. I declined. By this time Joe was storming down the road, waving aside the entreaties of his wife and her lover, and heading in the direction of the railway line.

Flo came running up to me as I stood in my doorway watching Joe as he steamed by.

'Bob, Bob, do something. He's going to throw himself under a train. We'll get the blame.'

I shook my head. Joe was carrying a suitcase. Would-be suicides do not usually bother to pack their spare clothes for the trip to the next world. I reckoned Joe was admitting defeat but was hiding it by making a dramatic departure aimed at causing the maximum worry to the victors.

And so it turned out. Subsequently, Joe did call a few

times in order to see Ishbael. He frightened Flo by muttering that any court could give him the custody of Ishbael because of Flo's immorality. He then obtained digs with a middle-aged widow who took a great interest in him, and thereafter his visits began to decline.

Meanwhile the bond between Flo and Ritchie grew stronger. It was as though she had to demonstrate that she could remain in love with one man. In the street they would walk arm in arm. When I called at their home, they would often embrace each other and emphasize how much they were in love. Both saw solicitors to initiate divorce proceedings so that they could be free to marry. Flo's emotional needs were satisfied. In Ritchie she also had a man who could do the odd jobs, as well as bring in a regular wage.

Feeling in the street continued to run high. Neighbours openly laughed at the sight of Flo and Ritchie cooing over each other in public. They were subjected to many sarcastic and biting comments. Flo reacted by withdrawing even more into the house. She even stopped going to the shop and just sent the children with a shopping list. She continued to keep a well-run home and to show affection and concern for her children. But I knew she felt restricted and I tried to find a way to draw her into the community again.

This came about through Mr Blenkinsop, a widower in his eighties who lived a few doors from Flo. One day, when passing, I heard his shouts and discovered him stuck on his toilet. The increasing severity of his arthritis meant he was sometimes unable to move for hours, yet he was determined to resist any attempts to push him into an Old People's Home. I discussed this with Flo and she began to look in every other day. A friendship developed between them. Flo began to cook him a midday meal. The friendship not only benefited Mr Blenkinsop, it also changed neighbours' attitudes towards Flo. Gradually the condemnation died away.

Flo also gained something else for, as she said to me one day, 'It's good for me to help him. For too long I've regarded myself just as a wife and mother. Now I feel I can give something to other people and that makes me feel better.'

Flo and Ritchie making their peace with the neighbourhood was a step forward. But the feelings of Fiona, Mac and Ishbael still worried me. When she told the children that Ritchie would be replacing Joe, Flo had also taken the opportunity to add to Fiona and Mac, 'Anyway, Joe's not your real father, so it doesn't matter.' They bombarded her with questions, but she declined to say more. Little wonder that Fiona became even more disturbed and Mac started to wet his bed – which roused Flo to fury. After Joe had left for good, Ishbael began to pine and say she wanted 'daddy Joe not daddy Ritchie'.

Flo worried about the children and one evening she called round and poured it all out to me.

'Bob, what shall I do? The kids have never been like this before. Sometimes Fiona looks at me as though I was a tart. And I can't bear to hear Ishbael sobbing. I love Ritchie but I sometimes wonder if I've made a terrible mistake. If it would make the children happy, do you think I should ask Joe back?'

I was moved by her words but pointed out that Joe's return – after all that had happened – would hardly solve the worries of Fiona and Mac. And if Flo was unhappy with Joe their relationship might break down yet again, so causing more strain for the children. My advice was to let Ishbael see Joe regularly and, in the meantime, for Ritchie to give her as much attention as possible. This approach worked and, within a few months, Ishbael seemed her old self, even though Joe's visits became less frequent.

With Flo's agreement, I made the effort to see more of Mac. The youth club had organized a sponsored buggy race in order to raise money for a set of football shirts. Ritchie provided some wood, I found some pram wheels and Mac and I co-operated to build a buggy. Once it was completed, the many slopes of Edgely ensured plenty of practice runs for our machine. So we enjoyed great fun – and danger – together. In the evenings, Ritchie joined in and it pleased me to see his hand on Mac's shoulder as we trudged back up the hill with the buggy in tow behind us.

One morning, as Mac and I were making some adjustments

to the wheels, I took the opportuntiy to say, 'You get on well with Ritchie.'

'Yes, I like him. And mum does . . . But he's not my dad is he? He can't be my dad. I thought Joe was my dad. Bob, why didn't mum tell me before? Now I keep thinking, who is my dad? Who am I? The other day, I was walking along the street when I saw a man who looked a bit like me and I thought, he could be my dad. My dad could be a murderer, he might be mad. And why didn't he want me?'

The length and intensity of Mac's speech displayed the depths of his feelings. I put aside the spanner and sat on his doorstep before replying.

'I know this has been bugging you, Mac. Your dad was a soldier. He was married to your mum for about five years. The reason he left was because he and mum didn't get on. It was not because he disliked you. In fact, I've heard her say he loved you. I don't know why he stopped visiting you after they split up. Sometimes dads love their sons but think it's easier for them and the mums if they don't interfere. But if it really troubles you, it might be possible to find out more about him, if your mum agrees. All that happened years ago. The important thing now is that Ritchie has really taken to you.'

Mac continued to spin the pram wheels as he listened.

'It's funny, Bob. I wasn't all that upset about Joe leaving. I can remember sometimes wishing he wasn't my dad, 'cos he didn't seem to like me. What upset me was how mum hid the truth from me all those years. It was as though she couldn't trust me with it. I like Ritchie. I want to love him like mum does. Perhaps he can take the place of my dad. If not, I know I can always ask you about my real father.'

He paused. 'Now let's give the buggy another run. Come on.'

We lost that buggy race but the time we had spent together building the machine was worth a hundred wins.

Seeing how unhappy Fiona was, I also wanted to speak to her. My attempts were rebuffed with an unaccustomed bluntness. At this stage, Flo and Ritchie sometimes went to play skittles for a pub team to which Ritchie belonged. Flo would not leave Mac and Ishbael on their own in the house and, considering Fiona's recent attitude, was unwilling to put Fiona and Legs in charge. I suggested that they invited Ruby Curtis in as well and paid all three for baby-sitting. Ruby was an old flame of Legs' but she remained a friend of Fiona and I reasoned that she would act as a kind of chaperon.

Unfortunately, the plan came unstuck. The next morning, Mac asked me to call round. I found Flo and Ritchie in an indignant mood. The skittles match never started as the opposition failed to arrive, so they returned home much earlier than expected. As they entered, Fiona and Legs had jumped up from the settee where they had been entangled while Ruby – buttoning up her blouse – had emerged from the kitchen with Stirling Drift. I couldn't help thinking that Stirling must make a habit of being caught with his girl friends.

Ritchie had bundled Legs, Ruby and Stirling out of the door, and a slanging-match between Flo and Fiona ended with mum giving daughter a few clouts. Flo and Ritchie were furious, not only about the behaviour of the teenagers, but with me for suggesting Ruby. I was tempted to ram Flo's hypocrisy down her throat. She had made her play for a number of men over the last few months and yet here she was loudly complaining about the permissiveness of the teenage generation. However, judging that her strong words probably reflected her concern for Fiona, I held my tongue. But the incident built a barrier between us. Perhaps Flo was looking for one now that she was starting a new life with Ritchie. Perhaps she genuinely lost some confidence in me. I continued to see the children frequently and sometimes dropped in to see her. But I felt that she did not value my opinion as much as before. Perhaps that was to the good. She could not always be dependent on me.

Oddly enough, the incident healed the breach between Fiona and myself. I was returning home one summer's evening when a figure stepped out from the shadow of a hedge. It was Fiona. She swept the auburn hair out of her eyes and announced, 'I've been wanting to see you, Bob. How about inviting me in for a coffee?'

I was pleased to comply and Bet – who got on well with Fiona – joined us for the drink. Fiona opened up.

'I want to say sorry for the trouble I caused you the other night. Mum used to think the world of you and now she blames you for letting Ruby and Stirling lead us astray. It's not fair. You've done so much for her – and for us.'

I dunked a biscuit in my coffee and let her continue.

'I suppose it was my fault. I didn't want Ruby playing gooseberry. I knew she fancied Stirling, so I suggested she invited him in. Nothing happened between Legs and me. We were just snogging. I let him have a feel but I won't let him go too far. Anyway, mum practically accused me of raping him. I told her she had no right to talk to anyone about morals and it ended with her hitting me. I probably deserved it. She's forgiven me now and you're the one who is taking the blame.'

'Don't worry about that, Fiona,' I answered. 'I'm pleased it's got us talking again. You seemed to freeze up over the last few weeks.'

She nodded. 'It's difficult to explain. I've always respected mum. She's brought us up strictly and even taught us that we're a shade above people around here. Then she started tarting herself up, going to discos, acting like somebody twenty years younger. She brought Ritchie in. It was horrible. And then having Joe back at the same time. It was like a pantomime, with the neighbours all laughing and sneering. When I protested, mum said it didn't matter about Joe 'cos he wasn't our dad anyway. I suppose I did freeze. I hated all adults for a bit. I wanted to hurt mum. I wanted her to think that I was sleeping around so that when she challenged me I could say – well, I'm acting just like you.'

Bet poured out some more coffee. 'Tonight you look like the old Fiona', she said. 'What's happened?'

A slow smile spread across Fiona's face as she replied, 'You won't believe it but Mac and I have been getting quite matey. He told me about the talks he had with you, Bob. He explained about our real dad. I understand a bit better

82

now. And I've tried to think what it's been like for mum. She's been through hell. Hardly any money, Joe moving away, that terrible court case, all the street against her. No wonder she wanted a man. It's coming out all right now. We've all grown stronger.'

5
Webster

Red Moore dragged out his old cricket bag. 'Take it,' he smiled. 'I bet the kids around here would love a game.'

Now that we had the kit, the next question was where to play. The only flat ground was at Blackway which involved a drive and possible conflict with the gangs there. We decided to play on 'the hill'. Just to the north of St Matthew's was a slope where people walked their dogs and viewed the town. The slope was too steep for sport. And a public toilet at the lower end of the slope reduced the possible play area. But for all its disadvantages, the hill was the only available ground, so it became our pitch.

A pattern developed: we played cricket every Wednesday evening and sometimes on Saturdays. Red's gear could hardly be described as up-to-date. The pads were just canes bound together by straps – they might have been worn by W. G. Grace. The bats were too large. The boys were puzzled by the abdominal protector, until Jules Thomas improvised by strapping it over his elbow. There were no stumps, so we made do with wooden boxes.

The slope of the pitch meant that on the downward side runs could be scored very quickly. Don Plumb, for instance, would use his powerful arms to score a fifty in boundaries and so avoid having to lug his bulk from one end to another. By contrast, it was almost impossible to hit the ball very far up the upward slope. On one occasion, Drew Sprite did strike the ball in that direction and began to run. The ball stopped, then rolled back down the hill, hit the other wicket, and so ran Drew out. The fact that he was probably the first batsman in the history of cricket ever to run himself out was of no comfort to the disgusted Drew, who promptly smashed the wooden box and stormed away.

The season witnessed some enjoyable games, with enthusiasm running high. The only 'inconvenience' concerned the public toilets. The stronger boys, particularly Don and Jardine, sometimes smote the ball directly into the loos. Usually we had to persuade a girl to retrieve it. Once we had to flee as an enraged female emerged, pulling up her knickers, and hurling both the ball and abuse at us.

The local schools frequently had days off for what was known as 'teacher training'. When the junior school closed for a day, I suggested a cricket match. The game was progressing well when I spied Webster watching from the side. I was surprised, for the secondary school was not on holiday.

At the close, I asked, 'Webster, what are you doing here?'

'I walked out,' he retorted. 'I'm not going back. I don't care what they do. They're always picking on me.'

I took him home and, over a cup of tea, his side of the story emerged. He was due to do catering – the only course he enjoyed at school. His regular teacher had promised that Webster could try his hand at a birthday cake for his mum's forthcoming birthday. Unfortunately, the teacher was away at a conference and a student teacher took over. He insisted that the whole class made jam tarts. Webster made his protest by refusing to don the regulation white overall. A slanging-match ensued, with the teacher saying that he must either put it on or get out. Webster went.

I realized that Webster should still be at school and that, by taking him in, I could give the impression that I was encouraging him to play truant. With his reluctant permission, I phoned Webster's school and spoke to his head of year. I had met Mr Black before: firm but fair. I was impressed by his interest not only in the academic high flyers but also in what were called 'the dumbos'. He was pleased to know that Webster had come to me but his version of the story was more serious. It appeared that Webster had pushed a desk over and landed a kick on the student as he rushed out. For the second time he was under suspension, and a letter was on the way to Sandra Summerfield.

I put the phone down and recounted the contents of our conversation. Immediately Webster blew up.

'That's right, believe what they say. I'm always wrong. That pratt of a student gave me a shove and I fell against a desk. I don't suppose old Black Boy told you that. And I bet he never said that he called me a "lazy toad" and said that the likes of me shouldn't be in a normal school.'

I calmed Webster down by producing the picture we had drawn the first time he had been suspended. Again I went over his problem of exploding when reprimanded by someone in authority. I explained once more that he had to control himself, even when he was unjustly accused, and then find a more effective way of answering his opponents.

Something in what I said got though. Webster's mood suddenly changed to depression.

'What's wrong with me, then?' he groaned. 'I'm always blowing my top. I do it at home, at club, at school. I wonder if I'm a nutter and ought to see one of those special doctors, a psycopath I think they're called. And what's my mum going to do when she finds out? You think I've got a temper. You've never seen her in a rage.'

The prospect of viewing the bulky Mrs Summerfield in a mild temper let alone a rage was enough to spur me into action. I began to consider ways of repairing the damage. I suggested to Webster that he immediately wrote a letter of apology to the student teacher. Predictably, he refused. I got him to write down what would happen if his suspension continued. He would miss the catering course; he might be sent to another school; his mum would break him into little pieces! I then placed an envelope against his list and said that putting a letter in the envelope was a small price to pay in order to avoid such consequences. He grinned and – with some help over spelling – wrote the letter.

The following morning, I dropped in to see Mr Black. He was pleased about Webster's letter, even though he realized that I had inspired it. The student teacher accepted the apology and the school authorities agreed that Webster could return the next day. However, Mr Black was not optimistic.

He pointed out that this was just another in a series of incidents.

'Letting him back in won't solve his problems. He's aggressive. He has a reputation as a thief. His truanting is becoming so bad that some teachers think he should go to court.'

Webster went back the next day. But Mr Black's pessimism was justified. Battles with teachers became daily occurrences. His willingness to go to school continually wavered. With his mum's consent, I would call to check that he was attending. If he was still in bed, I dragged him out. We almost came to blows. He had not expected such firmness and caved in. From then until the end of term he attended regularly, even though he tended to arrive late.

Leaving school did not solve Webster's troubles. He had a reputation amongst the other youngsters for being dishonest. During that summer his thieving reached a pitch that almost seemed beyond control. Clearly the youth club café was not making a profit. Webster claimed that members were nicking sweets while his back was turned. They were convinced that he was dipping his hand into the cashbox. Dylan and I therefore introduced a kind of auditing system. After each club we undertook the tedious task of calculating which items had been sold, how much money taken, and where the losses were occurring. Webster sulked, saying we did not trust him. But it worked. The losses did not recur.

Perhaps because this source of income was now denied him, Webster's shoplifting became more extensive. He would appear with new gloves, pens, scarves and tool kits and, under intensive questioning from me, would grudgingly admit he had nicked them. I refused to grass on him but made it clear that he was heading for trouble. Once, when out with me, I caught him nicking a padlock. To his embarrassment, I insisted on taking him back to the counter to pay for it.

Webster was crazy to possess a motor bike or car. He had ridden a friend's moped and was forever wanting to drive the minivan. One evening, walking down Muddiford Grove, I came across Webster crouching beside the front of a car. I thought he'd been waiting to pounce on me so, with a smile, I invited him in for a coffee.

'No thanks.'

'Grief, I've never known you to refuse. What's wrong?'

'Nothing.'

'Well, why are you kneeling then? Who are you hiding from? Are you in trouble with your mum?'

'No, you twit,' whispered a reddening Webster, 'I've got my finger stuck.'

Peering close, I realized the truth. Webster had been trying to open the bonnet of a car and finished with his finger jammed in the radiator grill. Eventually, I pulled his finger out and took him home. Despite the seriousness of the problem I could not help but see a funny side.

One day Mrs Battle's house was burgled. Mrs Battle and Webster did not get on – perhaps because they both had loud mouths and quick tempers – and she was convinced that he was the thief. Not only had the house been broken into and the rent money taken – but tea, sugar and milk had been splattered on the kitchen walls. Mrs Battle's rather outsize knickers and bras had been tied together and hung out of the bedroom window. Her empty bottles of whisky and sherry had been stacked on the doorstep in a milk crate. Nothing which belonged to Mr Alf Battle or the boys had been touched.

It didn't take a Sherlock Holmes to deduce that the culprit was a local person who disliked Mrs Battle. She called the police and voiced her suspicions. The first I knew of the incident was seeing Webster bundled out of his house and into a police car by two burly policemen. My attempt to intervene was met by a curt request to mind my own business. I immediately phoned the police station where an inspector agreed that Webster's parents should be present during any questioning. I promptly found Mrs Summerfield and took her to the station. Under questioning, Webster vehemently denied the charges and the police reluctantly let him go.

On returning home, Mrs Summerfield and Webster, accompanied by Flint, tore over to the Battles and started a flaming row, with most of Edgely gathering as the audience. Flint was ready to use his fists. Sandra used words that even I had never heard. Webster swore violently and declared that Mrs Battle was trying to frame him. The spaniel ran round in circles, barking and snapping at both sides.

Fangs, Syd and Johnson Battle were ready to take up Flint's challenge and advanced into their front garden. Mrs Battle's vicious tongue was responding in kind to that of Sandra Summerfield. For some reason, the verbal conflict shifted from the burglary to the faults of each family.

Sandra called Mrs Battle a 'drunken slut' and told Alf that if he were a man he would stand up to her.

Mrs Battle retorted that at least she could keep a husband and if Sandra wasn't such a 'fat ugly cow' Mr Summerfield wouldn't have been jumping into bed with all the tarts in Edgely.

I stood like a tennis umpire with my head shifting from side to side in an effort to keep pace with the verbal volleys.

Alf Battle began to look decided ill, so I thought I had to intervene. Taking his arm, I led him back into the house and then persuaded his wife that he needed quiet and a cup of tea. I ushered the boys inside and turned to accompany the Summerfields back into their home. Honour was satisfied on both sides.

Whatever his involvement in the Battle theft, it was still obvious that nicking had got a grip on Webster. On one occasion, he admitted that the row of biros in his shirt pocket had been stolen. I determined yet again to talk it out with him.

'Webster, why do you do it? You don't need those pens.'

Sometimes when I probed Webster angrily refused to talk. But this time he was in a mood to speak. He removed one of the pens and deliberately snapped it in half.

'No, I don't want them. I can't explain. I used to do it for a laugh. I liked the feeling of wondering whether I'd be caught. I enjoyed playing up the detective in Woolworths. Once my mum sent me to buy some socks. I bought them, then put them back and let him see me take them again. He chased me all down the street. When he caught me I showed him the Woolworth's bag and the receipt. You should have seen his face. But most of the time I really was nicking.'

'Do you steal from Mr Moore's shop?'

'No, what do you take me for?' Webster retorted in indignation. 'And I wouldn't nick from my mum, either – not like some kids do.'

'So why from Woolworths and the big shops?'

'Well, they can afford it. And why shouldn't I? Look at the money other people have got. Just walk around the shops in town and you see 'em spending hundreds on stereos, colour TVs, fur coats. Why should they have so much while my mum can't even afford a TV licence?'

I was silent for a minute. It *was* unfair that some had wealth in abundance while the likes of Mrs Summerfield struggled on a pittance to bring up a family.

'I agree that life's not fair. Perhaps we should be more involved in politics to see that the money does get shared out more. But that doesn't make nicking right. And supposing you are caught and sent away. That's not going to help your mum.'

It was Webster's turn to be silent. He sat picking at some scabs on his arm.

'The truth is, I can't stop,' he whispered. 'I want to stop. I tell myself how daft it is but then I do it. I keep thinking about taking a motor bike or a car. Not to keep, just to have for a bit, just to know what it's like to have your own wheels.'

He couldn't stop. The inevitable followed. One evening he broke into the school. A neat professional job. He glued some paper over a window to soften the sound of breaking glass. He put his hand through to undo the catch. He wore gloves so as not to leave fingerprints. He took two tape recorders and money from a cashbox while wisely not taking some cheques which he knew would be difficult to cash. But, incredibly, he played around with a typewriter and, on a nice clean sheet of paper, typed his name. It was as if he wanted to be found out.

The next morning, the school secretary discovered the theft and summoned the police. Before the morning was over, the police had called at his home, found one of the tape recorders and taken him and his mum to the police station, where he was formally charged.

Mr Black was almost as upset as I was. Although Webster had just left school, he arranged for him to see the schools' psychiatric service. He argued that a psychiatric report might persuade the court to deal more leniently with him. To my surprise, Webster agreed to Mr Black's suggestion. I recalled Webster's own words, 'I wonder if I'm a nutter.'

Mr Black made an appointment for Webster to see Dr Justin Walker. I offered to make a report available to the psychiatric therapist but he declined my offer. So, one afternoon, I deposited Webster at the clinic and arranged to meet him later at a cafe. He returned two hours later, his face flushed with both anger and amusement.

'That joker is a bigger nut than me,' he exploded.

'What happened, then?' I asked, shoving a cup of tea across to him.

'Well, he asked me all about my mum and dad. I expected that. Then he asked if I was keen about motor bikes. I told him I was just like every kid in our street. Then he showed me a lot of drawings and asked me what they were. I said tits because they were. Then he wanted to know if I had wet dreams. I said only when the roof was leaking. He was sex mad. Asked me if I liked masturbating when I stole things. And, when I asked him how I could stop stealing, all he did was to ask me what I felt about it.'

By the end of his account, both of us were laughing. Oddly enough, the interview did seem to do some good. Webster concluded that, as he was not on the same wavelength as the nutty therapist, he must be sane.

Although I did not share the intensity of Webster's views, I was forced to agree with his general assessment. This opinion was confirmed when, a few days later, Mr Black showed me a copy of the report which Dr Walker was submitting to the court. After an introduction about Webster's background, it read:

> Webster's stealing, aggression and immaturity stem from the absence of a father and the presence of a

dominating, overwhelming mother. Webster feels captured by his mother and longs for the love of his father. His interest, indeed obsession with motor bikes is an expression of his desire to prove he is an independent man, not a child dependent upon his mother. The motor bike symbolizes power and when Webster sits astride one – in reality or in his imagination – it becomes an extension of his penis, his manhood.

In stealing, Webster tries to find love. In our consumer society, material possessions have come to stand for love. So when Webster steals he is saying, I want the love of a father.

It is difficult to know what to recommend for Webster. A qualified therapist could cure him but it would involve intensive weekly sessions lasting for perhaps two years. In this period, his unresolved conflicts about love and power could be brought to the surface and mature mechanisms for dealing with them developed. However, I am sure the costs of such treatment are beyond the pocket of Mrs Summerfield. If he were younger, I would recommend that Webster be sent to a boarding school for the maladjusted. There a psychological environment would allow him to regress to the point in time when his father left him so that therapeutic help could enable him to deal with the trauma. Perhaps Mrs Summerfield will marry again and so provide a stable, mature, father figure for Webster.

'What rubbish,' I said to myself. 'To think he is paid a fat fee for this pseudo, high-sounding, clap-trap.'

No doubt, I was over-reacting. I was peeved that Dr Walker had not mentioned my efforts to help Webster. Even so, the report was so unhelpful. I agreed that his bad behaviour was connected with his feelings for an absent father. I knew Mrs Summerfield's child-rearing methods were not always suitable. I could have told the court that for nothing! But the report offered no concrete advice on how to help Webster overcome his problems.

At least the wait for the therapist's report meant that the

court hearing was delayed for a month. During this period, Webster went job hunting. He had no success but at least he was trying. Further, in that month, we kept a daily log of his activities and I was convinced he did no further stealing.

The court had also requested the Social Services Department to submit a social report. Accordingly, the Department sent Ms Joey Stackpoole to visit the Summerfield household. Webster liked what he saw of Joey. Tall, with blonde hair, she wore long flowing dresses and sandals. I had previously met her when I was invited to a social workers' lunch in the town centre. Her father was a retired naval officer and she had been educated at a leading girls' public school. She laughingly confessed that she became a social worker in order to ease her middle-class guilt feelings. Despite her background and a voice that would have suited a BBC2 cultural arts programme, Joey possessed an enthusiasm, zaniness and concern that was captivating.

After seeing Webster on the day before his court appearance, she rushed up to consult me.

'Look, Bob, I still haven't prepared this court report. Been completely taken up with showing solidarity with a residents' strike in the Old People's Home. Then there is a barmy barber who insists that baldness is a compulsory fashion – he's got to be certified today. So I've forgotten all about Webster. Be a dear and put me in the picture.'

I started to tell Joey what I knew about the Summerfield family. After a mere ten minutes, she jumped to her feet.

'Must go. Just remembered I've got to attend a case review in the Children's Home. By the way, be a dear, would you come to town on Saturday morning and give me a hand selling *Militant Monthly*? All this social work is just like a bandage, you know, it doesn't cure anything. The real object is to get rid of the ruling class.'

I grinned, 'I'll give you a hand when you decide to sink that ruling class admiral known as your father. No, on Saturday I'm due to play cricket with the boys. See you in court tomorrow, if the revolution hasn't started by then.'

The revolution did not occur, so the following day Sandra

Summerfield, Webster and I made our way to the juvenile court. Unlike the adult court, the juvenile section did have a waiting-room. Triangular in shape, its small area was packed with youthful defendants, their parents and witnesses. With so many people smoking incessantly, the windows jammed tight, the radiators on full blast (apparently they were turned off in the winter), it resembled the Black Hole of Calcutta.

Every so often, a solicitor, dressed in an expensive suit with a silk handkerchief in the top pocket, would emerge from a small room to advise his client how to plead. The 'clients' were so overcome by the occasion that they inevitably accepted the advice as a command. In addition, probation officers, clad in suits of a cheaper cut, and social workers, dressed in jackets with leather patches, would come to read their social reports to the defendants. The reports were supposed to be confidential but all the onlookers listened avidly. At the end, the youngsters and parents were asked if they agreed with the contents. Too embarrassed to prolong the agony, they all nodded.

Webster was spared the public report, as Ms Stackpoole did not rush in until we had been ushered into the courtroom. After the charges had been read, Webster immediately admitted the offences. The chairman of the bench was Mr Senior, the owner of a local furniture shop, who had a reputation for firmness combined with fairness. His colleagues were Mr Garth, a prominent trade unionist who took his legal duties very seriously, and a lady in a yellow hat whom I did not know.

Mr Senior then asked what was known about the defendant. Joey jumped up and pushed her report in front of the magistrates. As they quickly read it, Mr Senior asked whether Webster had seen a copy.

'No, not yet, your honour,' Joey panted.

She quickly handed Webster a copy and gave me one to share with Mrs Summerfield. I noticed with some satisfaction that she recommended that Webster should not be sent away.

The clerk of the court rose to point out the availability of two other reports. The one from Dr Walker I had seen. The other was from the school, but was written not by Mr Black but by Webster's class teacher. It pointed out that his class work was poor and his attendance had been irregular. The short statement ended:

'Webster Summerfield is a lout, a bully and a thief. There is little more to say.'

I felt myself reddening at these words. Combined with Dr Walker's recommendation, they were enough to get Webster sent to Devil's Island. I heard Mr Senior asking Mrs Summerfield if she had anything to say. Sandra rose to her feet.

'Yes, he is a good boy really, do anything for me around the house. He never gets into trouble and when he does I give him a good hiding. I blame the school myself. You cannot blame boys for breaking in when temptation is put in their way. You'd do the same, and what's more I don't see why you've picked on Webster. There's a lot worse than him in Edgely, so why aren't they here?'

Sandra Summerfield was working herself up. Under cover of the papers on my lap I gave her coat a tug. She ignored me and launched into an attack on the repressive police state. Fortunately, Mr Senior was equal to the occasion. He intervened.

'Thank you very much, Mrs Summerfield. Your remarks will be given very full consideration. Please sit down. Now Webster, have you anything to say?'

'No.'

'Stand up when you speak to the magistrate,' said the clerk of the court, giving Webster a friendly prod.

On his feet Webster extended his speech to, 'No sir.'

At this point, I felt I had to speak, and rose to request permission. After hearing of my contact with Webster, Mr Senior said he would be pleased to hear my comments. I began:

'Thank you, your honour. I very much regret what Webster has done. Nothing should be said to play down the seriousness of his offence. However, I would like to point out some of the more positive sides of his character. He has been a regular and loyal member of our youth club. He is in charge of the café there and has handled it very competently. There is one other incident to mention. Last week, our youth club held a bonfire and barbecue. A can of petrol fell over near the fire. Most of us ran away, but Webster dashed forward, put his coat over the can and removed it before it caught fire. By doing so, he may have averted a serious accident. So, despite the defects in his behaviour, I think it worth pointing out that he has many credits.'

I sat down. Mr Senior expressed his thanks and the magistrates left to ponder their decision. They were out for a long time. They then called in both the clerk and Joey Stackpoole to give them further information. Webster, convinced that the delay meant that they were going to send him away, was white and tense. His mum was red and blustering. I knew she would explode if Webster was taken from her care.

Eventually the magistrates filed back. Webster was told to stand up. Mr Senior spoke:

'Webster, you have committed some serious offences. In addition, your home circumstances and your behaviour at school do suggest that you would benefit from some corrective training elsewhere. However, we have given your case much consideration and instead we have decided to leave you at home but to make a supervision order for one year. This means that for twelve months the Social Services Department will supervise your behaviour. After discussion, it has been agreed that this supervision should be executed not by Ms Stackpoole but by Mr Laken, acting for the Department, providing Mr Laken is agreeable, that is.'

Mr Senior paused and looked at me. I nodded my willingness. He then continued:

'Don't think you are being let off. Mr Laken will submit reports to the Social Services Department and if you fail to toe the line you will be back here, and next time we may not be so merciful.'

As we filed out of the court, Mr Senior beckoned me over.

'I am glad to have met you, Bob. The Rev. Wantage has told me something about your work. I shouldn't really tell you this, but if you hadn't spoken today we would almost certainly have sent Webster away. You showed us another side of him. Anyway, Wantage was telling me that you hope to extend the Project after three years. I am sure the magistrates would be prepared to put in a plea for you.'

I left the court feeling considerably cheered and joined the company of a relieved Summerfield mother and son. The following days saw even closer contact between Webster and myself. Every day we looked at job vacancies, wrote letters and even attended a few interviews. I gave him mock interviews in an effort to improve his chances. But he was always turned down. Gloomily I concluded that his school reference, which every employer asked for, must be so bad that he hadn't a chance.

During this period, Sandra Summerfield was also more ready to talk to me. One day we discussed Webster as we sat in her kitchen. Sandra's methods for dealing with Webster alternated between two extremes. She either smothered him with attention and made every possible excuse for his misdeeds, or else she would thrash him with a belt. Webster was afraid of his mum and, despite his age, submitted to the beltings, but would react by sulkiness and depression which sometimes provoked him to further rebellion.

I put forward my view that Webster needed a middle way, that Sandra should acknowledge his faults, punish him when necessary (although not by corporal punishment) and constantly offer hin affection and encouragement.

Although Sandra and I could not agree about Webster's needs, we were now on much more friendly terms. As I left, she gave me a jocular pat on the back that almost landed me on the pavement. If Webster put up with her heavyweight beatings, I thought to myself, he really did love her.

Webster had forged a special bond with Bet. She enjoyed his cheeky good humour, his mimicking of her cockney accent and his obvious affection for her. He revelled in the concern she showed and the kind of semi-flirtatious relationship that developed. He would often stay for a meal, taking great delight in playfully criticizing our cooking. Like many youngsters on the estate, Webster's preferred menu was very limited. He liked fried chips, sausages, bacon, eggs and beans. He would not even try pizza or rice. And once, when

Bet served up new potatoes, his reaction was, 'I hate new potatoes, I like instant mash.'

Webster's birthday fell during these summer months. Apart from ours, he received only one birthday card – from his mum. His father no longer even remembered the day of his birth. Bet baked him a birthday cake and also asked Sandra down for a slice. When he saw the cake with its candles, Webster laughed and told Bet she had probably put poison in it. But as he cut the cake he fell silent and was near to tears. The four of us sat round the table for a game of monopoly. As usual, Webster began to corner all the property. He laughed when I landed on his hotels and was forced out of the game.

'Sorry dad,' he chuckled, 'but you've been beaten by a better player.'

Webster paused as he realized what he had called me. The game came to a momentary halt. Sandra, for once calm and reflective, said softly, 'I wish he had had a dad like you.'

My emotions suddenly welled up. For all his age, I wanted to take Webster in my arms. Yet I had to emphasize the truth.

'One day I might have a son like you. I am not your dad and I never can be. But you are very close to us. You are more than a friend.'

Webster was silent. Bet got up, bent over him and lightly kissed him on the cheek as she went out to put the kettle on. A slow smile spread over Webster's face and he stretched across the table and squeezed his mum's hand.

The mercy of the court and the strong relationship between Webster and us did not mean that his troubles were over. The temptation to steal or to erupt into temper tantrums remained. Every day we talked about it. Every day we sat down and recorded his victories and lapses. Then we got a break.

Clare Curtis was working lunch-times in a bar at the Richmond Hotel. She phoned me to say that the hotel's restaurant had a part-time vacancy for a kitchen hand. I immediately went down. To my surprise not only Clare but Blondie Blake was also behind the bar. I wondered who was looking after

Blondie's children. With their hair piled high, white frilly blouses and black pencil skirts, Clare and Blondie fitted the part of barmaid.

Clare, knowing I was looking for a job for Webster, had arranged for me to meet the manager, Mr Sellick. With droopy moustache, long sideburns, greying hair and a velvet suit, he was a cross between a Mexican bandit and Elvis Presley. As he approached, he squeezed Blondie's backside and she laughed, but once he was past she lifted her fingers and gave him a 'V' sign. He greeted me politely and told me that Clare and Blondie had already told him about my work.

'Lovely girls, Bob, lovely, so accommodating. If this Webster works as hard, I will be satisfied. It's an evening job, 7 p.m. to 11 p.m. five days a week. We provide free meals and a taxi home at night. The pay is good, and it could lead to a permanent post.'

The same day, I told Webster. He jumped at the job. He mostly washed up but the chef also gave him some tuition and gradually allowed him to undertake some cooking.

The satisfaction gained from working seemed to strengthen Webster's resolve to stop nicking. One Saturday evening, Bet and I were disturbed by a noisy banging on the door. Webster stood there panting and asked if he could come in. He slumped into a chair and explained that he had been trying car doors in the road. He had found an unlocked one and stood between temptation to drive a car and to go straight. Eventually, he tore down the road and sought refuge with us. I praised him for his strength.

Later, as he left, he said, 'I have been listening to Ted on Sundays, Bob. I have prayed hard that I will stop nicking.'

'I'm praying, too,' I added as I closed the door. I was thankful that with a job and some money in his pocket, Webster's life seemed to be entering a more stable phase.

My handling of Webster did not receive universal backing.

'You spend too much time with that Webster,' was Mr Plumb's comment. 'Just give him a thick ear, or he'll end up conning you.'

On the other hand, Dylan and Doreen Willis perceived

the battle going on within Webster and reckoned that my intervention could tip the scales and make him a decent citizen rather than a crook.

6
Blondie

Dylan and Doreen Willis had encouraged me to persevere
with Webster. And it was Doreen who was responsible for
my meeting someone who became almost as regular a caller
as Webster. Thus, a few days after his court appearance, I
opened the door to a woman who immediately apologized.

'I'm so sorry to disturb you. I hope you don't mind. Mrs
Doreen Willis said I should call on you.'

Her name was Mrs Helen Shaw. She lived in the same
street, yet this timid-looking woman had never said more
than 'good morning' to me. She was in an anxious state and
her eyes filled with tears.

'Please tell me to go if you're busy – but I don't know
what to do. I could never walk into the big welfare building
in town. I do know your face. Doreen has been so good to
me. She said you wouldn't mind me coming but I'm sure
you have more important things to do.'

By this time I had manoeuvred Mrs Shaw into the living-
room, sat her down and put the kettle on. As I handed her
a cup of coffee, she smiled. The smile changed her appearance and revealed an attractive face. I explained about the
Project and then asked her what was wrong.

'It's George, my husband. I'm sure he's carrying on with
another woman. He denies it but I can tell. Makes flimsy
excuses about working late. He's no time for me, no time
for the children. And he's not giving me enough money. If
he is working overtime, why is he earning less money? The
house is like a tip. He never decorates. The toilet needs
repairing.'

Mrs Shaw went on at length. George was her second
husband. The impending breakdown of a second marriage
made her feel a complete failure. She and George had two

children, Julie an eight-year-old who suffered from epilepsy and Francis, aged four. The medical needs of Julie and the emotional demands of Francis had become extra burdens with which Helen felt she was not coping. She wept and apologized for doing so.

I did little except listen. Yet having a man prepared to sit, listen and try to understand seemed important to her. I explained that Mr Shaw was legally responsible to support her and the children financially. I offered to speak to her husband. She declined.

'Oh no. He'd be angry if he knew I'd discussed our affairs with anyone.'

The conversation switched to the children, whom she loved dearly. I praised her for the sensible way she was handling her daughter's epilepsy. Helen glowed at the compliment. Obviously she did not receive many. We also spoke about Doreen Willis, who appeared to be her only friend.

'Doreen is a Christian,' she said. 'I suppose you're the same. I've always been an atheist but the atheists don't seem much help when you're in trouble.'

She rose to leave and I told her to feel free to come any time.

Helen took me at my word. She called frequently, giving me a running commentary on her troubles. Then she came in distress.

'He's gone. George has left me. He's moved in with his fancy woman.'

Helen sank down. For once she was silent. A mute despair took hold of her. I took her hand, for I had no words of comfort. Eventually she lifted her head.

'What's wrong with me? Two men have left me. What am I going to tell the children? How can I cope on my own? What will I do about money?'

'I've not got the answers, Helen. All I can say is that we are your friends and we are close at hand. If George has gone, we want to help you re-build your life – and the children's lives.'

'Thanks Bob, I only wish I had your faith.'

After that, Helen knocked on my door nearly every day. She continually brought me letters from her solicitor. They concerned divorce, custody, maintenance and access to the children. I sought to translate the complex legal jargon. Sometimes Helen reached a panic point, when she was convinced that the court would take the children away from her because she had twice failed as a wife. I was able to tell her quite definitely that any court decision about the children would be based on her qualities as a mother. I also said I was prepared to support her case.

At the same time, I attempted to sort out her social security claims. Helen felt humiliated at having to apply for assistance and her state of anxiety meant that she could not think clearly when faced either with a sheaf of forms or an inquiring official. So I sat down with her and wrote out her financial income and expenditure.

At other times, she called to borrow the phone, or to ask if I would run Julie to the doctors. Once she asked me to examine the TV set which she thought was going to explode. After a storm, I checked all the wiring in her home as she was afraid that water might seep on to live wires and cause a fire.

I was not the only person on whom Helen leant. Doreen Willis gave her affection, time and friendship. Then one morning, as Helen was leaving to prepare lunch, she paused and said, 'I'm the same as Doreen and you now.'

I hesitated, not sure what she meant.

'I'm a Christian,' Helen said. 'Doreen has shown me the way.'

She shut the door and scampered away.

I considered her announcement as I cooked some beans on toast. People would be watching her closely now. What if Christianity had no effect on her? I rebuked myself for my lack of faith. If Jesus Christ had taken on people like Ted, Dylan, Doreen, Bet and myself, why not Helen? He had love and to spare for the anxious and insecure.

What with Helen, Webster and Flo, I was fast becoming a one-man social services department. Neighbours were now frequently reporting matters of concern to me. I was told that Ruby Curtis was taking boys into her bedroom, that Drew Sprite had broken into the local garage, that Lionel was making a habit of nicking people's milk from their doorsteps.

If these problems reached me secondhand, others landed directly on to my plate – or doorstep. During the school holidays, the teenagers often dropped into our home. As well as playing swingball and drinking coffee, they liked to tinker around with my old typewriter. One afternoon, Lesley Curtis, who had seemed moody and down-hearted. inserted a piece of paper.

'I can't think what to type,' she grunted, as she rested her cropped head on her slim fingers.

'Type your life story,' suggested Bet, who was doing some dusting. Later she looked at the result. It read, 'Unwanted child. Dad a crook. Hopeless at school. Sisters hate me. Mum picks on me.'

Bet gave a rueful smile. 'That's a cry for help if ever I heard one. I'll ask her to give me a hand with some cooking tomorrow and see if I can have a chat with her.'

Meanwhile, Mrs Daphne Peters had fallen out with Jardine. Now fifteen, Jardine was beginning to throw his weight about in the home. He refused to wash, wore filthy clothes and was staying out late. Worse, he had been drawn into glue-sniffing. When Daphne discovered him inhaiing from a plastic bag in his bedroom, she had had enough. She told him he was as bad as his father and that he could sling his hook. Jardine swore at her, shouted that he didn't want to live with a 'nigger screwer' and stormed out, smashing a pane in the door as he went. Within four hours he discovered that being a gentleman of the road in pouring rain wasn't so romantic. He knocked on our door. Bet and I took him in for the weekend. It served as a cooling-down period. Despite the disagreements, I knew that bonds of affection did tie mum and son together. By Monday he was back home.

A listening ear, a warm home, a spare bedroom, enabled us to deal with these problems. With others, it was the help offered by neighbours which proved crucial. When Mrs

Sprite went into hospital for a minor operation, the limpid Mr Sprite could control neither the defiant Drew nor the energetic Jake. I had a word with old Mrs Barnes and she volunteered her services. Each day she turned up at the Sprites' at breakfast-time and stayed until the evening. Not only did she clean and cook but, more important, she also attempted to provide some of the firmness and affection so desperately needed by the two boys.

Aid from local residents was also built into the next development. The youth club continued to run at Labour's Studios. Apart from an occasional smashed window caused by the too-enthusiastic use of a billiard cue and the continuing graffiti on the toilet walls, Lew Labour had few complaints. However, the younger members moaned that the club was dominated by their seniors. Certainly, the likes of Troy Peters, Rebecca Willis and Mac Scott were not getting a look-in on the snooker and table-tennis tables. Moreover, some of the even younger ones, like Wally Blake and Ishbael Scott, were considered too small to attend.

Admitting the substance of their grievances, I started a junior club. By holding it on Mondays, from 5–7 p.m., it could be squeezed in at St Matthew's before the Whist Drive commenced. The only difficulty was that all the games gear had to be loaded into the mini-van and transported each week from the Studios to the church and back again. However, the willing co-operation of parents and teenagers in running the club more than compensated.

Helen Shaw started a craft table. Mr Alf Battle proved sufficiently patient to sit and play monopoly with a bunch of noisy scamps. Clare Curtis and Mr Plumb came when they could. Webster ran the café and Gail Curtis assisted with the craft activity. Jules Thomas and Jardine Peters attempted to keep order, although their strong-arm methods sometimes intensified rather than lessened the riotous behaviour of the young members.

The junior club, covering the seven-to-thirteen age-group, attracted large numbers. In the small church hall, the table-tennis player had to keep a wary eye on the dart-throwers. The snooker participants jostled with impromptu gym displays. Mrs Shaw and Gail Curtis utilized the stage, where they sat surrounded by glue, toilet rolls, cotton reels, paint and about twenty children clamouring for their attention. In one corner, Jules and Jardine tried to run a game of British Bulldog too close to the monopoly board. Chaos. But popular and enjoyable chaos. With such large numbers, it would have been impossible to run the club without the active and willing support of the parents and teenagers.

Wally Blake often arrived early at junior club and stayed as late as possible. He was also one of the youngsters about whom neighbours whispered their concern. About this time I had discovered Blondie working in the hotel. I wondered if her children were being left unattended. With Webster having taken up so much of my time, I had neglected to visit the Blakes. I now rectified this omission.

I knocked on Blondie's door. Wally opened it and yelled, 'Mum, it's Bob.'

Blondie shouted to me to come in. She was standing in front of the mirror, putting on her lipstick. High heels, a tight-fitting skirt, a green satin blouse, her blonde hair flowing down – even from the back she looked great. For a moment, I thought she must be working evenings at the hotel as well as lunch-times. Then I noticed a cigarette glowing in the corner. On closer examination, I made out a chunky male figure. He, too, was dressed to go out.

'This is Sandy – he's on the tarmac lorries. Sandy, this is Bob, my social worker. You've heard all about him.' Blondie gave me a squeeze as she disappeared upstairs.

'You do tarmac, then,' I stammered, trying to make conversation.

'Yer. We're doing a bit of the trunk road at the moment. Travel a lot. If you want your path tarmacked, I can use the firm's lorry at the lunch-break. Won't cost you much and I'll earn a bit on the side.'

'No, thanks. The council do the paths for us. How did you meet Blondie, then?'

'Oh, at the pub,' Sandy answered. 'Bought her a few drinks and chatted her up. I'm lodging with her for a bit.

My firm pays us a lodging allowance, see, and Blondie does me very cheap. That means I got some extra to take her out. Suits us both, temporary like. She's a good cook. Good at other things, too. She likes you.' This was accompanied by a knowing look.

'I'm mostly concerned about the children,' I responded rather primly.

'Oh, those little buggers. I'm always buying them sweets.'

Just then Blondie descended the stairs and lugged Sandy to his feet.

'Wait a minute, Blondie,' I protested. 'You're not leaving the kids alone?'

'No, 'course not. Steve and Molly are baby-sitting. Just keep an eye on them 'til they come. We're in the darts' team. Must go. Bye.'

I was left with feelings of worry and resentment. Worry about Blondie leaving the children, resentment that she should treat me like a servant. I couldn't leave the children, so I stayed. June was fast asleep. I picked up a book and began to read to Wally. Within twenty minutes the baby-sitters arrived on a motor bike. They turned out to be colleagues of Blondie's from the hotel. Steve, a porter, was about eighteen, with heavily greased hair. He immediately sat down and turned on the telly. Molly, dark-haired and heavily perfumed, was about a year younger. At least she spoke to me and I explained who I was. She told Wally to get ready for bed and, from her tone, made it clear that I could now leave.

My evening visit reflected a snapshot of Blondie's life. She worked lunch-times at the hotel bar, cleaned the house in the afternoon, and spent most evenings at the pub with a bloke. Sandy soon left but was replaced by others. While out, she made make-shift arrangements for neighbours and friends to baby-sit. Sometimes I feared that these arrangements fell through.

Anonymous phone calls to the police, the NSPCC and myself reported that she was leaving them unattended and that she was entertaining different men in the house. I always followed up the complaints but never found the children alone. At the same time, I had to admit that Blondie had made strenuous efforts to furnish the home, that the children were well clothed and that she always provided them with regular, well-prepared meals.

I wanted to have a long talk with her, yet every time I visited she either had company or was about to go out. Then she sent for me.

'Hi, Blondie. Wally says you want to see me. Anything wrong?' I tried to put a cheerful note in my voice.

'There's nothing wrong with me. It's this little punk.' She jerked a thumb at Wally, who had retreated to the door. Blondie was hunched over the kitchen table, her hands wrapped round a cup of coffee. Her hair was uncombed, an old dressing-gown was draped loosely around her. June, now over two, squatted on the floor, sucking a biscuit.

The scene reminded me of the one when I first met Blondie. She was a woman of moods, she tended to swing from the fun-loving teenager to the depressed, middle-aged housewife. Following these moods, her own appearance, her care of the children, the tidiness of the house, also swung from one extreme to another.

'He's been shoplifting, that's what's wrong. Twice Mr Moore has caught him nicking sweets. Says if he does it again, he's banned from the shop. He seems to blame me. Me! I give him money for sweets nearly every day. And I've had a note from the school. Here, see for yourself.'

Blondie jabbed a letter in front of me. The junior school head complained that Wally was inattentive, surly and sometimes walked out of school without permission. He requested Mrs Blake to come and discuss the matter.

'Now, Bob. You tell him you'll put him in a Home if he don't behave. The police will take him.'

I declined to threaten Wally. Instead I turned on Blondie. For days I had been storing up in my mind what I wanted to say to her and now it came out in a jargonized rush.

'I know you love Wally, otherwise you wouldn't have stuck with him all this time. But, Blondie, he must wonder why you go out so much. He must have doubts about your love. Perhaps he steals to test you, to see if you'll love him no matter how bad he is. And he needs more consistent handling. Sometimes he whines for a biscuit until you give in, other times you clout him. What's more, it can't be good for him seeing all your boy-friends. He wants one father to model himself on.'

Blondie's face tightened. Her white teeth parted in anger. I realized I had said too much, too soon. In an attempt to back-pedal, I praised her success in keeping the home clean. But it was too late.

'Don't you soft soap me, Mr high-and-mighty Laken. I asked you here to sort Wally out not to attack me. You've been going to that chapel too much. You religious types are all the same, too keen to point out the faults in others. Suppose 'cos you've been to college you think you're a brain surgeon with all your posh words. Well, when you've got some kids of your own, you can tell me how to bring up mine. Perhaps you're jealous because I've got kids and you haven't. Well, my advice to you is to go home and see if you're man enough to put your wife in the family way.'

I left, reflecting on the mistakes I had made. Still, I took some comfort from the fact that my words had at least prodded Blondie out of her mood of apathy.

The following Friday, Blondie phoned me from a call-box by the school. It was 5.30 p.m. and Wally had not returned. I jumped into the mini-van and we drove around searching and asking children if they had seen him.

'He said something about looking for his dad at the cemetery,' Rebecca Willis remembered.

'The cemetery?' I repeated in puzzlement.

Blondie groaned.

'Oh, he keeps asking about his dad and I've told him he's dead and buried.'

To reach the cemetery, Wally had crossed a busy main road. We sighed with relief when we spotted him peering at gravestones. Blondie rushed and embraced him.

'Wally, my darling, I thought I'd lost you. I was so worried. You know I love you. I want you home with me not in this creepy graveyard.'

Then she put him down and slapped him across the face.

'And that's for making me late. I've got a date tonight, you selfish little pig.'

Wally said nothing. He climbed into the back of the van, holding his face. We drove in silence until Blondie spoke.

'OK Bob, you're right. I am inconsistent. I must be doing something wrong if he wanders off like this. Will you come and talk to me on Monday?'

I nodded. I was also thinking of how I could talk to Wally.

Bet knew I was worried about the Blakes. On the Saturday, I didn't even listen to the football results. She pulled me out of the armchair and took me for a walk. I felt better strolling along with Bet's hand in mine. We talked as we sauntered. I went over my plans for helping Blondie, while Bet reacted with criticisms and encouragement. Somehow we finished up at Ebenezer Chapel. Ted always left it unlocked. He was held in so much respect that it was never burgled or vandalized.

We went in and sat down on a pew as we silently prayed and meditated. Despite its Victorian name, its hard seats and dowdy decorations, I had come to love the chapel. I went to the front and stood in Ted's place. In my mind, I saw the people who usually came there. It struck me that God had brought some of them through very hard times. I committed Blondie, Wally and June to his care and left feeling stronger.

The following Monday, I began my programme for helping Blondie. The idea was to develop a five-point plan over the following weeks.

Point one, it was essential to boost Blondie's confidence in herself as a person capable of being a good mother. I explained that her concern about Wally being late showed she really did love him. I praised the improvements she was making in the home. She had purchased some second-hand carpet for the bedrooms. She had persuaded Ted Williams to instal a fireplace. She had even started to tidy the garden.

Point two, we budgeted together. After putting down her income from social security and her part-time job, we then worked out her expenses. Not surprisingly, the results revealed that she over-spent on fags and the pub. I devised a system of putting money aside for the rent, fuel, food, clothes and other essentials.

Point three, we talked much about Wally and June. We tried to pinpoint what was behind Wally's bad behaviour at school and his wandering away. I explained that loving children was not the same as giving in to them. I encourged Blondie to express affection towards them as well as being firm in discipline. She was now ready to listen and even to put into practice some of the ideas. She tried not to give in to the whining for biscuits, sweets and money. At times, although with some reluctance, she cuddled Wally and read to him.

On one point I made no progress. I wanted Blondie to tell Wally the truth about his dad, as I reckoned the uncertainty was troubling him. Her tale about dad being dead had satisfied Wally in earlier years but now he was asking how he died and Blondie could not provide the answers. Other children in the neighbourhood were telling him stories about his real dad. I guessed that Wally's trip to the cemetery was in order to discover if his father really was buried there. Yet Blondie was adamant. She declared that she did not want to revive painful memories and argued that if her son knew the truth he would want to meet his dad.

Point four, I encouraged Blondie to talk about her own childhood, for I felt that something about it still worried her. She had already told me that, at the age of five, her mother had left her in the care of gran. She described gran's chaotic slum in the old flats in the town centre. She recalled how she spent much time playing in the streets. With unusual emotion, she expressed her gratitude to the kindly old lady who, for all her untidiness, had provided warmth and affection. Her shock and dismay was thus all the greater when, as a ten-year-old, she came in from school and found gran dead in a chair.

With no relatives willing to take her, Blondie was then removed to a council Children's Home. Soon after, her mother reappeared and started to visit her, usually accompanied by a small girl called Nora and sometimes escorted by different men. Blondie revealed how she longed for her mum's visits, yet wanted to hurt her. Blondie's loud mouth, temper tantrums and sexual precociousness meant that she was moved from Home to Home. Her mother angrily tried to persuade her to reform, warning Blondie not to be a slut. And all the time she was standing next to her latest boy-friend.

Then mother and Nora stopped visiting. Nobody explained why, although other children informed Blondie that her mother had murdered Nora in a drunken rage and had then committed suicide. Not knowing whether this was true, Blondie had felt unable to ask anyone. She left the Home at sixteen, with predictions that she would end up 'on the game'. Yet in her heart, she had been determined to make a decent home, one better than those she had experienced.

'I wanted my own room' she said, 'to cook my own meals, have a colour TV, a fitted carpet, just like the Home's super-intendent had.'

As Blondie talked, much of the pattern of her life became clearer to both of us. Her lack of possessions and experience of financial poverty had resulted in her commendable deter-mination to establish a materially decent home for herself and her children. The fact that she had never lived in a normal home meant she had never observed parents bringing up babies in a way she could copy. And her early sexual adventures had set up an expectation that men provided short-term gratification rather than long-term relationships. These long talks were a help but not a solution.

'I still dream about my mum – sometimes have night-mares,' she commented, 'I still want to know more about her. She's like a ghost that still controls me.'

Point five, despite the deeper understanding we were gaining about Blondie's past, I still had to warn her about the possible consequences of her present behaviour. While acknowledging her need for physical affection, I argued that the succession of men-friends was confusing to the children. I also made it clear that if the children were left unattended, the council might remove them to save them from possible dangers – from fire, gas leaks, or wandering off.

'You can't expect me to live like a nun,' Blondie protested. 'I can't be cooped up in the house all the time.'

A less nun-like person than Blondie was hard to imagine

– as I pointed out. I repeated that if she went out she had to ensure there were capable baby-sitters.

The warm respect between Blondie and myself was now such that she could accept my criticisms. I often explained that I had no right or duty to visit her, as I worked only for a voluntary agency.

'No, I want you to call, Bob,' she responded. 'It's good that you check on me. Keeps me on my toes. Anyway, I'd sooner have you than someone official from the welfare.'

Several weeks passed smoothly. I began to believe my plan was succeeding. Blondie had no man living with her, and when she went to her lunch-time job, or evening jaunts, she ensured that an adult neighbour came into the home. She seemed buoyant, almost bouncy. She delighted in telling me how she was dealing with the children, how she was decorating the bedroom and how 'pure' she had become. But it was as though she had climbed a mountain only to fall down the other side. Gradually, her moods became darker. She began to snap at me and the children. I noticed that she was bringing drink into the home. Her short-lived stability was about to take another change.

The first indication I had was when I made a routine 'pop in' to see that Wally and June were not alone. Such a call usually involved a tap on the window and a quick word with Mrs Plumb or Mrs Barnes or whoever was there. This time the downstairs curtains were drawn. There was no response to my tap. I waited and tried again. Then Molly drew the curtains and opened the window. Behind her, I could see Steve stretched out on the settee. Molly casually did up a couple of buttons on her open blouse. She flipped her black hair out of her eyes.

'Oh, it's you, Bob. Sorry. We were busy.' She laughed and turned to grin at Steve, who ignored us and lit a fag.

'Did you want to come in and investigate, Bob? What would you like me to show you? Mind you, Steve might not approve.'

A breeze blew back her hair and blouse. Molly stayed still,

enjoying her pose. Suddenly I felt angry. Angry that Wally and June should be in their care.

'What if Wally walked in and saw you?' I challenged.

Molly's mood changed.

'Well, he wouldn't see anything new. What do you think Blondie is, a virgin?'

I forced myself to be calm.

'Look, I'd like to check that the kids are all right. Will you let me in?'

Molly opened the door. She stood, hands on hips, as I went up the stairs. Blondie kept Wally and June in the same bedroom, to cut down on heating costs. June was fast asleep in her cot. Her face was unwashed and a bottle dripped by her side. Blondie still used a bottle to keep her quiet. Wally was also asleep but uncovered. He had wet the bed and lay in his own urine. The bed-clothes stank. I could find no clean pyjamas, so I changed him into a dry vest and pants. I removed and replaced the wet under-blanket. He hardly stirred.

The bed-wetting did not concern me at that moment. It often happened and I attributed it to Wally's general sense of insecurity. What did disturb me was the lack of cleanliness in the room. For all her faults, Blondie had been keeping both the children and the rooms in a tidy state. I wondered if her actions could be interpreted as neglect and whether the time had come to ask the Social Services Department to take action. Would the children he happier and safer if they were separated from Blondie? Yet I knew that strong feelings of affection tied them all together. I grasped the edge of June's cot and asked God's protection for them and his wisdom for myself.

As I descended the stairs, Molly emerged. She was now properly clothed.

'Sorry, Bob, I was a bit rude to you then. You just came at an inconvenient moment.'

'That's all right, Molly. Sorry I was so sharp. I'm all tensed up today. You'll stay until Blondie returns?'

'Of course. And don't worry about Wally catching us.

I've told Steve he's on starvation rations for the rest of the evening.'

I grinned, tousled her hair and left.

The two following days were taken up with the exploits of Webster. Then, just as I was about to leave for the youth club, Blondie phoned me from a call-box. Her voice was slurred. At first I thought she was drunk.

'It's no good, Bob, I'm cruel. I'm useless. I'm going to finish it.'

The line went dead. I called to Bet to ask Dylan to look after the club. Jumping in the van, I sped to Blondie's. The front door was open. She was stretched out on the stairs. Wally was shrunk in the corner as though hoping that the walls would engulf him. June was screaming upstairs. I guessed what had happened. In the bathroom, I found an empty tablet bottle.

Pausing only to ask the next-door neighbour to keep an eye on the children, I tried to carry Blondie to the van. She was heavier than I thought and I had to drag her, until Mr Plumb happened to come by and helped me lift her. Within ten minutes, I was at the hospital. The receptionist, as was her fashion, treated us calmly.

'Hmm. Attempted suicide. We'll pump her out.'

While Blondie was taken off, I gave the receptionist details about her doctor, address, date of birth and family history. Then a young doctor beckoned me and asked what kind of tablets she had taken. I handed over the empty bottle but it bore no markings. The doctor shrugged, as though I was to blame. I waited.

It struck me that Blondie would not have phoned me if she had really wanted to kill herself – unless the call was to ensure that I cared for the children. So much for my great five-point treatment programme. I wondered what else I could have done. What effect would the trauma have on Wally?

My doleful thoughts were interrupted by a nurse, who informed me that Blondie was safe, that I could not see her, that, as a matter of hospital routine, she would be interviewed by a hospital psychiatrist in the morning, and that I should phone in the afternoon.

Wally and June stayed the night at our house. Fortunately, it was half-term, so Bet could look after them the next day. In the afternoon, after phoning the hospital, I visited Blondie. She looked tired and haggard. For all her good looks her face presented a picture of the drawn middle-aged woman she would soon become.

She took my hand and whispered, 'I couldn't help it, Bob, everything happened at once. I'm behind in the rent. Yes, I spent it on booze and I couldn't face telling you. Then I got the sack. Old Sellick accused me of dipping into the till. I came home and the kids wouldn't stop screaming and whining. I kept saying no to Wally and he bit my hand. I snapped. I picked up the wooden spoon and began laying into him. He just stood there. I thought I would kill him. I couldn't go on. I rushed upstairs and swallowed those tablets. When I became drowsy, I thought I had to tell you. I don't know what would have happened to me if you hadn't come. Are the kids all right? Will they be taken away from me?'

'They're with Bet at the moment. The doctors say you need two weeks' rest. If you agree, I'll get them into a foster home until you are better. In the meantime, I'll sort out the rent. You just take it easy.'

'Thanks, Bob. You are a friend. I don't like it here – all the others are old people.' Blondie paused and, for a moment, her eyes lit up with some of the old sparkle. 'Mind you, one of the doctors is real nice. He's examined me three times. I think he fancies me.'

I left and made my way to the Social Services Department. The co-operative Area Manager, Roger Driscoll, listened carefully to my story. He already possessed a large file on Blondie which he somehow managed to skip through as he listened to me. Pushing back his spectacles on to his balding forehead, he remarked, 'I reckon you're saving us work. If you hadn't dealt with Mrs Blake, we would have been called in. What do you suggest now?'

My suggestion was that Wally and June be fostered with Mrs Barnes until Blondie recovered. I knew that if the process went through these official channels then the Social Services Department could pay Mrs Barnes for her efforts. I argued that it was better for the children to go to her than to some unknown foster parent.

'Hm, very irregular. See, Mrs Barnes is not one of our approved foster mothers and we are not allowed to pay unless they are on our official list.' The area manager paused. 'But the alternative might mean taking the children into a Children's Home, as we are very short of foster mothers. I guess we could approve Mrs Barnes on the strength of what you say about her. However, Wally and June will have to be received into the care of the local authority, otherwise we certainly cannot pay. I'll get Miss Stackpoole to run the forms up to Mrs Blake to sign. One last word, we've had a number of complaints about Mrs Blake. If she doesn't improve, we may have to remove the children on a more permanent basis.'

Leaving the Social Services building, I drove up the hill and back to Edgely. I dropped into Mrs Barnes's and, as I anticipated, she was delighted at the prospect of looking after the children. I returned home to find Bet serving tea to Wally and June. As we stuffed ourselves with egg and chips, I explained to them that I had seen mum, that she was getting better and that they would stay with Mrs Barnes until Blondie was fit again. They knew Mrs Barnes well and seemed pleased at the opportunity to stay with the lady they called 'old gran'.

After tea, I went upstairs to help Wally pack the few possessions we had stuffed into a plastic bag when leaving his home. I also took the time to look more closely for any signs of the beating Blondie had imposed. I noticed two small bruises on the back of his thigh. Nothing else. I asked him how he had collected them.

'Oh, I had a fight at school and a boy kicked me,' he lied. I grinned, not at the lie but at his loyalty to his mum. Then, as I was transferring his pyjamas to a canvas bag of mine, I came across one of Blondie's dresses. The shiny, bright red garment was stuffed under his pillow. For a moment, I had

117

visions of an eight-year-old transvestite. Wally noticed my discovery.

'I wanted something of mum's,' he muttered. 'I thought that if I never saw her again, I could think of her when I saw the dress.'

I picked him up, held him tight and carried him out to the mini-van. Bet followed with June. They received a warm welcome from Mrs Barnes. Bet lingered for a cup of tea while I nipped back to the hospital to let Blondie know what was happening.

Blondie remained in the hospital for a further three days. On the second day, I took Wally and June to see her. I had wondered whether the sight of their pale mum in a hospital bed would upset them. However, I decided it was more important for them to maintain contact. June was obviously delighted to see mum. She wee-d on the floor again and jumped into Blondie's open arms. Wally found it much more difficult to express his feelings. He sat close to his mum, not holding her but clutching her pillow. His anxious eyes darted around the hospital ward. I noticed him staring at the very old lady who was breathing heavily in the bed opposite.

Afterwards, we drove back in the mini-van. June sat beside me while Wally squatted in the back. We passed the cemetery where I had found him just a few days before. The sight of it obviously stirred something within him.

'Bob,' he asked softly, 'will I stay with old gran for ever if mum dies and is put in there with dad?'

I could see his white knuckles clenching the back of the driver's seat. I tried to choose my words carefully.

'Your mum is not going to die, Wally. Like I said, she'll probably go home tomorrow and when she is better you and June will go back to her. But just suppose something did happen to her. Well, I'd be around to make sure that someone nice looked after you.'

Wally said no more. He kissed me on the back of the neck. Aggressive, tough, deprived – Wally actually kissed me. I realized I had gained his friendship and trust. At that moment, I wouldn't have swapped my job for anything.

118

The following day, I transported Blondie back to her home. While I lit the fire and put the kettle on, she walked all over the house, going into each room in turn. She was pleased to be home. We poured the tea and sat and talked about all that had happened. We agreed that Blondie would walk around to Mrs Barnes's each day, to show the children that she wanted to see them. She realized that her suicide attempt had upset Wally and she promised that in future she would contact me when she felt desperate. I arranged to drop in every day for the coming week.

'Bob, I want to ask you something but I don't know how to say it.' Blondie filled my cup for a third time as she struggled with her words. 'I sometimes wonder if my mother's badness has come into me. When I hit Wally that time, I could have been a murderer like her. People say cruelty runs in the blood. I'm scared that I'll batter one of the kids. When I was in hospital, I had nightmares about it.'

I was shaking my head in disagreement.

'No, Bob, try to understand,' she continued, before I could speak. Her face was tense and worried. 'Consider the facts. My mum had more men than hot dinners. She left me with gran. She couldn't have loved me. Then she murdered Nora. I'm just like her. People call me a tart. You're always lecturing me 'cos I neglect Wally and June, so I suppose I don't love them. And one day I'll lose my temper and do something terrible. Just like mum.'

Blondie paused for breath as her eyes met mine, as though expecting to find an answer there.

'Blondie, you're so wrong,' I countered. 'I agree that everyone's behaviour is partly shaped by what goes on in their childhood. We've been through all this before. But nobody is a duplicate of their parent. OK, I have been worried about some of your handling of the kids. I do think it wrong that you have so many men. On the other hand, I know you love Wally and June. I've seen how worried you get about them. You missed them so much when you were in hospital. And I truly admire the way you've stuck with them despite all the difficulties you've faced. You can be different from what has gone before. What's more, I'm not so sure your mum was as bad as you paint her. You don't know for definite that she murdered Nora.'

'Bob, I must know the truth about my mum. It hangs over me all the time. Will you find out for me?' Blondie pleaded.

I believed she had the right to know the facts about her past, so I set about seeking them. Roger Driscoll gave me permission to look up Blondie's childhood file. After some searching, a young clerk tracked down the records of Brenda Turner, as she was originally known. The file went back to the time when the Children's Department was responsible for deprived children. I opened the faded, bulky brown folders. Bits of paper fell out and I spent some time shuffling them into order.

I discovered that young Miss Turner (Blondie's mum) first came to the attention of the Children's Department in the 1950s, when she was pregnant. The Department's child-care officers gave her some nappies and a lecture on the dangers of VD. They then helped her obtain a place in a Mother and Baby Home, where the baby was born. For the following five years, Miss Turner staggered from unsavoury digs to seedy boarding-houses, often losing them because of the noise made by her baby. When the child, Blondie, was five, Miss Turner arranged for her to be cared for by a Mrs Tiler. The Children's Department had a loose kind of responsibility for such private fosterings and an officer occasionally visited. After the annual visits, the officer usually wrote that she was concerned about the age of Mrs Tiler, worried about the disappearance of Miss Turner but satisfied with the good intentions of the elderly foster mother.

In 1962, the reports began to fill out. Mrs Tiler had died, Miss Turner could not be traced. Blondie was taken into the care of the local authority and placed in a Children's Home. I began to skip through the pages, pausing only to read some fascinating snippets. I read of Miss Turner's reappearance with another daughter, Nora. I learnt of Blondie's misbehaviour, which caused her to be classed as unsuitable for fostering and to be moved from Home to Home.

Then, when Blondie was thirteen, her mother ceased to call. Reports about Blondie became less frequent. However, annual review reports were made about every child and the one for 1965 contained a reference to the tragic death of Miss Turner. Nothing was said about murder or violence. Hastily, I read on but could find no more details. Unfortunately, it appeared that no one had ever explained to the teenage Blondie what had happened. Perhaps the officers had considered it best to shield her from the pain of death.

Returning the file, I left the council offices and ran the hundred yards or so to my next port of call – the headquarters of the local newspaper. If a sensational death had occurred, it would have made headlines. A helpful assistant produced the papers for 1965 and I began to thumb my way through. I found nothing.

Deflated, I returned to the Social Services Department. Another idea. The officer signing Blondie's last reports was a Miss Roberts. Perhaps she still worked there? Roger informed me that she had retired years ago. However, he knew her address, phoned her, explained who I was and handed the phone to me. Miss Roberts certainly remembered Miss Turner and explained that she had died – tragically young – of cancer. Nora had not been taken into the care of the Children's Department because her father – not the same as Blondie's dad – had claimed her. Miss Roberts's latest information was that Nora had gone to live with her dad in a farm labourer's cottage. I thanked the old child-care officer and put the receiver down.

'So she wasn't a child murderer.' Blondie's eyes were taking on something of their old shine as I recounted my detective work. 'And I bet it was because of her illness that she couldn't visit me very often. You know, Bob, she probably wasn't such a bad mum after all.'

'No, and the same applies to you. Come on, we're due to collect Wally and June.'

We drove the short distance to Mrs Barnes's home. As we

went, I wanted to point out to Blondie that she felt better after discovering the truth about her mum and that it was inconsistent for her to withhold knowledge about his dad from Wally. However, the time did not seem right. We drew up, Wally and June rushed out and jumped into the van. Blondie thanked Mrs Barnes and gave her a box of chocolates. Dear old Mrs Barnes replied that she had enjoyed having them, even though she now felt worn out. She promised to call in each week to see Wally and June.

Autumn arrived. Wally was back at school. June's name was down for the day nursery and Blondie was promising herself a part-time job once she started there. Mrs Barnes babysat when Blondie went out. Blondie seemed to have more confidence in herself. But, as so often, appearances flattered to deceive. I was watching TV one evening with Webster when Don Plumb and Fangs Battle knocked with some 'exciting news' which they were prepared to trade for a cup of coffee.

'All right, what's your world-shattering piece of news?' I asked, expecting some irrelevant story like Don having decided to become a brain surgeon.

'Butter Martin's moved in with Blondie Blake.'

'Who?' I queried in my innocence.

'Butter the nutter,' exploded Webster. The boys went on to tell me that he was nicknamed Butter because of his skill at head-butting in pub brawls. The 'nutter' bit was added because he was considered mad. He had just been released from prison after serving a term for robbery with violence. I groaned as I considered that he was just the macho type to appeal to Blondie.

'Bob, I warn you. You must stay away from Blondie's now.' Don said these words with an earnestness that showed he was really worried about me. I was touched but knew I couldn't keep away.

7
Lorna

That summer and autumn seemed full of people competing for my attention. It also witnessed a diminishing contact with old Lionel.

He had continued as a regular visitor to our home. He would knock and request, almost demand, a cup of tea and a sandwich. As he ate, his eyes would roam around the room deciding what other items he might beg. Lionel, more than anyone else, really tested my Christian practice. Most people on the estate, I liked. Lionel began to arouse feelings in me of revulsion. Mr Finch, his landlord, had described some of the old man's habits, his refusal to use toilet paper and his smearing of faeces on the walls. Lionel rarely washed and carried around a smell so strong that it lingered for hours after he had left. He was light-fingered and pots of jam, bags of sugar and bottles of milk began to disappear from our kitchen. Worse, sometimes his hands would stretch out to touch little children and I began to wonder if he was a danger to them. Even Bet, who was cheerfully tolerant of the bawdy remarks of men on the estate, told me that she could not bear the feeling that Lionel was mentally undressing her. Yet, as a Christian, I knew I must show him love and not withdraw from him.

Suddenly, the Lionel affair came to a head. At 2 a.m. one morning, I was awakened by a furious knocking on the door. Lionel stood there. His lip was bleeding, and around him were stacked about twenty cardboard boxes and carrier bags. Mr Finch, having reached the end of his tether, had evicted Lionel and helped him on his way with a punch in the teeth. Lionel was all for summoning the police in order to lay charges. I calmed him down, pointing out that in the past the landlord had exercised tremendous restraint.

Lionel slept on the couch, and first thing in the morning, I took him to the Housing Department. He was reluctant to go, saying he was prepared to put up with the couch for a few weeks, but I insisted. To my delight, the housing official, Mr Ridgeway, again turned up trumps. Lionel carried no rent arrears, for he had never before been the tenant of the council. He was homeless and there happened to be a vacancy.

The same day, I transported Lionel's belongings to a one-bedroomed flat in a tenement block in the centre of town. The walls were unpapered, the floor was dirty, several windows were cracked. But it possessed a cooker, a bath and an indoor toilet. Together we toured the second-hand shops for cheap furniture. Lionel was pleased and I left him happily fiddling around with the gas ring, a saucepan and a tin of beans.

After that he never knocked on my door again. Edgely was too far away from the town centre for him to walk. Occasionally, I would visit him to share a dirty cup of tea and to leave him a parcel of food or clothes.

The day after moving Lionel to his flat, I had the opportunity to rid my system of his and the town's smells. We went to the seaside. The idea originated with Ruby Curtis, while the youth club was spending its second holiday at Butlin's. She suggested that we should have an outing for everyone in Edgely. I took up her proposal and on the last day of the school summer holidays took over a hundred people in two coaches for a day trip to the sea. Elderly folk like Mr Blenkinsop and Mrs Barnes came, as well as parents and children.

The elderly members were content to stretch out in deck-chairs under the September sun. The teenagers made a bee-line for the amusement arcades. Mr Plumb and his cronies slipped off to the pub. Mrs Roly Williams, Miss Bird, Helen Shaw and a few others, ventured to explore the shops. The smaller children built sandcastles, in between stuffing themselves with candy floss. The slimmer mums – led by Toni and Clare – donned bikinis and pretended to be annoyed by the pesterings of passing males. The bulkier mums, with

124

Sandra Summerfield and Mrs Battle for once acting in unison, tucked dresses into their bloomers and paddled in the sea.

The day drew to a close and we reluctantly returned to the coaches. Speeding through the countryside, a sing-song developed. We sang a mixture of old favourites, pop songs and nursery rhymes. We played 'I spy' to amuse the infants. Mr Plumb's request to stop at a pub was out-voted on the grounds that most people were skint.

However, we did agree to Troy Peters' urgent pleas to stop as he was bursting. His need to attend to the call of nature had a psychological effect on nearly every other boy in the two coaches. Within a minute, over thirty lads were standing in a long line against a hedge, quite oblivious to the cat-calls shrieked out by the rest of the party. I was thankful that no girl initiated a similar pattern for the females. We moved off again and I settled back, feeling so tired that I ignored the sight of Clare's bikini top, tied to a fishing-rod, being waved from the coach in front.

Tired or not, I had to leap into action again when Johnson Battle declared his intention of vomiting. I had never been a boy scout but I had come prepared. Jerking out a plastic bag, I handed it to him. The sight of Johnson throwing up began to have an effect on stomachs full of candy floss, ice creams and greasy chips. Others followed suit. Although not classified in medical textbooks, puking epidemics are the bane of distraught outing leaders. Fortunately, the adults met the challenge by opening windows, mopping up with paper tissues and producing containers which varied from plastic cups to beer bottles.

At the end of the journey, I clambered down the coach steps and thankfully breathed in the Edgely air. But my day was not over. Dylan emerged from the other coach, escorting a boy whom I did not recognize.

'Hello, I didn't know you'd brought a friend with you.'

'I didn't,' replied Dylan. 'He's not one of ours. He got on the wrong coach.'

'Oh, no,' I groaned. 'I've heard of losing kids on an outing but not finding an extra one.'

The boy, aged about eight, was beginning to cry. I told him not to worry and ascertained that he lived about thirty miles away. I phoned his home and brought joy to a very worried mum. His dad was still searching for him at the seaside so I offered to drive him home.

As I endeavoured to start the mini-van, Lorna Thomas asked if she could come for a ride. The Thomases had all been on the outing. The family now extended to three generations. Mrs Becky Thomas, despite the scene she had created at the announcement of Lorna's pregnancy, had accepted baby Elvis into the household. She now stood nursing him, while encouraging Lorna to accompany me.

Having safely returned the lost boy to the grateful arms of his mother, Lorna and I began to talk on the return trip. Her relationship with Stirling Drift still had all the stability of a yoyo. Mrs Thomas was enraged that he had still not contributed one penny towards his son's upkeep. At her insistence, Lorna had started legal proceedings to claim maintenance from him. The case was due to be heard the following week and Lorna wanted me to go along with her. I agreed.

I had become accustomed to the crowded court waiting-room. With the know-how of an old hand, I secured seats for Mrs Thomas and Lorna on the edge of a radiator. Lorna, looking nervous, nursed baby Elvis.

Stirling Drift entered, followed by his mother. He elbowed his way through the throng towards us. Lorna greeted him with an expectant smile. Pulling out a comb, Stirling smoothed his greasy black hair into place while admiring his reflection in the window. He casually lit a cigarette for Lorna and began to chat her up. Her was certainly a charmer. His winking and grinning were followed by whisperings into her ear which prompted peals of laughter from the simpering Lorna.

I groaned, telling myself that Stirling was about to persuade her to withdraw the maintenance claim. Mrs Thomas looked out of the window in disgust. Then Stirling tried to take hold of the baby. Lorna held on.

'Come on, Lorna, love. Let me nurse him for a bit.'

'No, you'll make him cry.'

'Don't be daft. I'm his father. I've got a right to hold my own baby.'

'Oh, is that so?' responded Lorna, her mood changing. 'If you're so interested in your baby, why don't you come and see him? If you care about us, why not help out with some money?'

'That's right, Lorna,' piped up Becky Thomas. 'He's only interested in one thing and it's not babies.'

'Belt up, you old hag,' snarled Stirling. 'Why don't you go jump off one of your stars, or drown yourself in a bottle of brandy?' Turning to Lorna, he continued, 'Don't tell me what to do. That's your trouble, you want to own me, always telling me when to come, what to wear, how much to spend. Anyway, I don't care. He's not my child.'

'What do you mean, he's not your child?'

'How do you know I'm the father? I wasn't the only one who had you. I heard that when you were at Butlin's you slept with so many redcoats it's a wonder the baby isn't a red indian.'

'I like that,' exploded Lorna. 'You're the one who's been laying it around. I've never touched anyone else, you liar.'

Their loud voices attracted the attention of other people in the room, which now became the stage for a theatrical display. Lorna and Stirling were the star performers, their mothers the supporting players, myself a minor actor and other clients the audience. The latter lost interest in their own cases as the fascinating details poured out.

Stirling delivered a passionate soliloquy which painted Lorna as a cross between a harlot and a baby-batterer. She responded with a colourful speech which described him as a mixture of Bluebeard and Hitler.

I made feeble efforts to divert them into talking about the latest football results, into sucking polo mints or into changing the baby's nappy. They verbally pushed me aside and continued their drama. Both were near to violence and I envisaged Lorna throwing the baby into Stirling's wide-open mouth. He was in full flow, declaring that he would rather spend the rest of his life in prison than pay a penny to Lorna, when the usher summoned our case into the magistrates.

The change of environment seemed to transform Stirling's personality. The roaring lion became a meek lamb who admitted paternity, gave details of his finances and agreed to a maintenance order to be paid weekly into the court. He and Lorna then left the court hand in hand, leaving Mrs Thomas holding the baby and me wondering if I would ever be able to understand their behaviour. Becky Thomas sighed with satisfaction.

'That's the financial problem sorted out. I don't think we'll have any more worries for a bit.'

Despite her knowledge of the stars, Becky's prediction could hardly have been less accurate. One week later, I was again called to the Thomases' household. Jules was sent outside. Bernard actually switched off the TV – so I realized something serious had occurred. Lorna, her lips pouting in vexation, sat nursing the baby. Becky Thomas ran her fingers through her dyed blonde hair, poured herself a brandy, and said one word.

'Again.'

'Pardon?'

'Again. She's done it again. She's pregnant again.'

'Not by Stirling, surely? They're always quarrelling.'

Mrs Thomas was beside herself with rage. She almost screamed.

'Yes, by Stirling. What's it matter what they keep on saying to each other? It's what they do when they're not quarrelling that counts. Oh, Bob, two babies by the age of sixteen. What can we do?'

'I couldn't help it,' Lorna suddenly shouted. 'I couldn't remember to take those pills. Anyway, he said I wouldn't get pregnant if we did it standing up.'

'Standing up, standing up,' shrieked her mother. 'What are you, some kind of sex pervert? I suppose you've been doing it standing up in the bus queue.'

Unable to retrain herself any longer, Mrs Thomas jumped

to her feet and twice cracked her daughter round the head. She stopped when Lorna used baby Elvis as a shield. She then raged on about the promiscuity of the young. Meanwhile, her co-habitee, Bernard, took the baby and handed Lorna his large, dirty handkerchief. She dried the tears which were falling from her large eyes.

'Well, you're not staying here,' Mrs Thomas thundered. 'You can clear out and take your bastards with you.' She pointed dramatically to the door. Standing here, draped in a long black robe, she somehow reminded me of Lady Macbeth. Now it was Becky's turn to be in the centre of the stage, I thought, smiling a little.

'What are you smiling at, Bob?' she interrupted. 'It's not funny. I thought that with your religious views you would be the first to condemn immorality.'

I rose to that one.

'Listen, Becky, Christians may know what wrong behaviour is but that doesn't mean they have to treat people as outcasts. You felt like this when Lorna first became pregnant. OK, I'm not saying there will be room for her when she's got two children but please don't kick her out now. She needs you.'

It was Becky's turn to sob.

'All right, Bob, I didn't mean it. But I just don't know how to cope any more. All the neighbours will gossip about us. I feel so ashamed. And it's hard enough managing with the money now, let alone with all the preparations for a new baby.'

She sat down and seemed to withdraw into her black cloak. Bernard put a comforting arm around her.

At 7 p.m. the following evening, a worried Mrs Thomas gave the familiar, hard, urgent knock on my door. She explained that, after the row, Lorna had not uttered another word. She'd got up early that morning, taken baby Elvis and had not been seen since.

'I'm frantic, Bob. It's so cold out. What about the baby? I've been to Stirling and he hasn't seen her. I've asked all over Edgely. She's run away. It's all my fault. She's hardly any money. What will happen to her?'

Becky's face was worn with anxiety. I ran her home in the mini-van and told her to rest a while. Lorna sometimes sat in cafés in the town centre, so I promised to search these. I drove rapidly to the town pausing only to drop into a couple of snack bars. No success. Nor had she been seen in any of the other cafés. I searched the amusement arcades. I even asked at the railway station if a young mother and baby had boarded a train that day.

'Yes, mate,' answered the ticket collector. 'About twenty of them. Has your missus left you, then?'

Lorna had had little money, so I decided she was not likely to have caught a train. The autumn evening was darkening and a cold wind prompted me to button up my jacket and turn up the collar. If Lorna was in town, I reckoned she would seek somewhere warm and cheap. But what warm place would be open so late? Then I had it. Lorna had recently taken to borrowing romantic novels from the library. Leaving the car at the station, I ran to the new municipal library. The lights were still on. She was there. Huddled against a radiator she had Elvis beside her in his carry-cot. She buried her head in my coat.

'Oh, Bob. She said she was ashamed of me, ashamed of her own daughter. I couldn't stand those horrible looks. I couldn't even speak to her. I had to get out. I've been so miserable and cold.'

'Sh. Quiet, please. This is a library not a public house,' hissed a ferocious-looking librarian.

Picking up the carry-cot with one hand and putting the other around Lorna, I guided her outside. We drove back while I explained how worried Mrs Thomas had been. Lorna now felt guilty at having caused her mum so much worry. I plonked her on the door-step, where another tearful reunion took place, and wearily departed for bed.

During the next few days, I made frequent visits to the Thomases home. Lorna was determined to keep the new baby and would not consider adoption. Mrs Thomas was once more busily consulting her charts and books in order to ascertain what kind of character the new arrival would possess. She now declared that she would never throw Lorna out but did argue that their council house would be too cramped once yet another baby was added. Anywhere more unlike a council house was hard to imagine. With a paraffin heater always on, strings of beads catching your ears at every move, baskets hanging from the walls, it was more of a cross between Aladdin's cave and the Amazon jungle.

But it certainly was overcrowded, so I took Lorna along to see Mr Ridgeway at the Housing Department. The difficulty, he explained, was that although Lorna had a clear need for accommodation, she was not of sufficient age or income to warrant a council tenancy. Lorna began to cry softly. With her long eyelashes fluttering as the tears fell, her big sloe eyes cast downwards, her large lips trembling, her arms cradled around her baby, Lorna's appearance was enough to melt the heart of Scrooge. Mr Ridgeway was no Scrooge and he seriously wanted to help. He thought for a few moments and then looked something up in a file.

'Hm, this could be the answer. Edgely has two council houses with grannie flats built on to their sides. One of them is due to be vacated soon. It needs a committee ruling to authorize a change of use but I'm prepared to recommend to the committee that this house be allocated to the Thomas family.'

The enterprising official's idea was that Mrs Thomas, Bernard, and Jules should live in the house, with Lorna and the two babies occupying the flat. Becky and Bernard were prepared to move and, to our delight, the Housing Committee did accept Mr Ridgeway's proposal.

'Never say that councillors haven't got a heart,' I grinned at Lorna, when she showed me the letter which conveyed the good news.

'No,' she replied. 'And if Stirling does want to marry me, he can move into the flat.'

From this remark, it was clear that Lorna still wanted to continue her liaison with Stirling. He remained as annoying as ever. One day he would be seen arm-in-arm with Lorna as they pushed Elvis round the estate. The next day, he would be tearing along on his motor bike with another girl behind him. My efforts to persuade him to stick with Lorna were met with colourful replies – all of which, interpreted, meant 'Mind your own business.'

One evening, our kick-about game of football continued until late. The game ended in á draw. Everyone then took a penalty – still level. So we decided to have what we call a 'killer goal' – first team to score wins. Feelings ran high and the boys defended as though the world cup was at stake. At the finish, we were playing under floodlights – well, the street lamps and the headlights of passing cars. We tramped home, tired and muddy, our hot breath sending streams of vapour into the cold night air. Turning into the road where the Thomases lived, we halted. Lorna and Stirling were having a ding-dong of an argument.

Standing outside Lorna's gate, they were engaged in a loud, rude, vocal controversy that would have been a credit to two politicians. The themes ranged over the familiar ground; Stirling raged away that Lorna was bossing him around and that her mum was always interfering; Lorna complained that Stirling was not paying any money and had been seen snogging with another girl. Her fair hair was blowing across her face, her eyes were wild, and her full lips mouthed obscenities. She was hardly recognizable as the sweet, retiring girl I had known on the Butlin's holiday, or the demure, quiet young lady who had sat so modestly in Mr Ridgeway's office. Suddenly, she leapt at Stirling and clawed his face with her long finger-nails. Stirling retaliated with a slap around the ear which sent Lorna sprawling.

Windows were thrown open. Neighbours appeared at doors. Mac Scott pranced up and down, yelling, 'A scrap, a scrap, a scrap.'

A crowd soon gathered, like some old-time prize-fight. The boys seemed to be on Lorna's side.

'Go on, Lorna, hit him where it hurts most,' shouted Webster Summerfield. 'Stirling, Stirling, Stirling,' chanted Ruby Gail and Lesley Curtis – no doubt hoping to win his favours by their vocal support.

Lorna's small frame seemed to have expanded. She leapt

132

upon her lover, and her weight forced him to stumble over the kerb. As he fell, she gave him a terrific kick in the groin. The crowd cheered. Embarrassed and pained, Stirling lashed out with his feet and fists but Lorna refused to give way. She spat into Stirling's face and yanked out a handful of his greasy hair. He retaliated with a fearful blow to her stomach.

The blow made me remember that Lorna was pregnant. I had been so fascinated by the scene that I had lost the will to intervene. Mr Plumb acted before me. He lunged forward and parted them, holding each combatant in his strong arms.

'I don't mind a fair fight,' he growled. 'But man against woman ain't fair.' He pushed Lorna in my direction and advised me to take her indoors. He warned Stirling that if he troubled a girl again he would receive his size twelve boots up his backside. I thanked Mr Plumb, just as he had once thanked me. He had shown me what I should have done as soon as the fight had started.

Stirling Drift did not reappear. The reason for his absence was not just the warning from Mr Plumb. His meek submission in the court had been replaced by boasting bravado outside. He refused to comply with the court order to pay maintenance. As if to cock a further snook at the magistrates and the Thomases, he had been strutting around in a new bomber jacket, bright blue jeans and high-heeled cowboy boots. The court responded with a warning letter and then a summons to appear before the magistrates again. At this point, Stirling took to the road. His mother said that he had fled to relatives in Newcastle. She insinuated that the strain of coping with Lorna, and of Mrs Thomas's efforts to separate him from his baby son, had been too much for him. Poor Stirling.

At least Stirling's departure meant that Lorna was not for ever chasing after him. Becky and Lorna drew close together as they prepared for the next addition to the family. Further, the council informed them of the date they could move to the new house. Bernard borrowed a mate's open van and on a cold, fortunately dry, November day, they carted their belongings along the two streets to their new abode.

I gave them a hand. Bernard and I managed the heavy

furniture, Becky dragged out her books, Lorna dealt with the baby's belongings, while Jules and his mates carried the light goods. With furniture piled high and small boys hanging on the sides, the van resembled a life-boat with survivors fighting to stay on. The van made it and the unloading was completed with the help – or hindrance – of the boys.

The granny flat was built on the side of the house. It consisted of just one room with a wash basin, plus a toilet. Lorna was pleased because it gave her a certain amount of independence from her mum yet retained a physical nearness. I left them that evening with Mrs Thomas untangling her curtain beads, Lorna planning how to decorate her room, and the worn-out Bernard snoring on the settee.

The Thomases were going through a smooth period. The only disturbance concerned the behaviour of Jules. Lorna came to complain about him.

'He's getting out of hand, Bob. He's just wild. He threatened to hit mum the other day. And the way he glares at Elvis. He thinks that babies shouldn't cry. Bernard does nothing about it, he just watches TV and sleeps. Jules gets away with murder, he won't wash up, he stays out late.'

I refused to believe that Jules had been transformed into Attila the Hun. I pointed out that he always stuck up for Lorna when her reputation was brought into question by other youngsters. Nonetheless, I had to admit that he was going through a rough patch. I determined to speak to him, and an opportunity arose when he was helping me to clear up after youth club.

'You've been looking fed up lately,' I started as we carried out the snooker table. 'Do you feel that Lorna, Elvis and the coming baby have taken over your home?'

'No, of course not,' he replied. 'Well a bit. Yes, I've had a bellyful of it. I'm fed up with mum giving all her time to them. It's "Don't disturb the baby", "Turn the telly down", "Lorna has got to rest". It's all women and babies in our home. They decide everything. I wasn't asked if I wanted to move. And Bernard is just like an old woman.'

'So you think you've got to throw your weight around a bit to show you're a man?'

'I suppose so.'

'Well, Jules, I sympathize with you. I don't know how you put up with the smell of nappies all the time, the baby yelling his head off and Lorna smashing Stirling to smithereens.'

Jules chuckled. 'That was great. She really taught him a lesson. Oh, it's not so bad really, Bob. I know mum's had a lot of worries. It's just that I feel so hemmed in at times and I want to kick out at someone.'

'Tell you what, Jules, next time you feel fed up, don't take it out on them. Pop into my place and I'll give you that game of darts I promised you. There are no smelly nappies in my house and no babies.'

'OK, Bob,' he laughed. 'I'll do that. But only if Bet cooks me some of her mince pies.'

The conversation with Jules by no means turned the Thomas household into a haven of harmony. Nonetheless, it did help and Jules would sometimes drop into our house to explain how he was getting on, as he munched one of Bet's pies or biscuits. The Thomas family sorted itself into some form of peaceful co-existence. Christmas passed uneventfully and in January, the new baby arrived. He was born prematurely, so he and Lorna had to spend extra time in hospital. Bet and I went to visit the proud mother.

'What are you naming him?' Bet asked, as I stared at the shrivelled scrap of humanity.

'Clint', Lorna replied. 'After Clint Eastward of course. He's gorgeous.'

'Good job your favourite film star wasn't Groucho Marx,' I quipped.

'Imagine that, Groucho Thomas. Still, the way he's yelling now he is a bit of a grouch.'

Lorna returned to her flat. She found it hard bringing up two babies both of whom had strong lungs, were in nappies and lacked the presence of their father. Lorna was the kind of girl who liked to sleep late in the mornings and she'd relied on her mum to do much of the caring for Elvis. Now – whether by accident or design – Becky decided it was time she went out to work and obtained a part-time post at a new bookshop in town called Erotic Literature. It specialized in books on magic, the stars and sex – all of interest to Becky. One result was more money for the Thomases. Another was that Becky had less time to look after the babies.

Faced with two demanding children, no news from Stirling and few opportunities to get out of the home, Lorna felt the strain and, at times, got near to severe depression. Fortunately, a sympathic health visitor called regularly. Dr Keen was always willing to discuss the children's health. Probably most vital, though, was the support given by some of the neighbours. In particular, Mrs Plumb, who lived in the same street, and Toni Hale, who loved to nurse babies, dropped in regularly. They helped with some of the chores, gave tips on baby care and sometimes took Clint and Elvis out for a walk while Lorna either put her feet up or escaped into town.

I reminded myself that Lorna was still a teenager, and reckoned she wasn't doing so badly after all.

8
Helen, Drew and Phil

The Thomases were not the only children with whom I welcomed in that new year. In January, I stood as god-parent for Julie and Francis Shaw. Mrs Helen Shaw had taken her conversion to Christianity with the utmost seriousness. Relating well to the Rev. Charlie Wantage, she attended services at St Matthew's. She had been along to Ebenezer Chapel a few times but found the services too disorganized and haphazard for her taste. She preferred the order and symbolism of the traditional Church of England services.

That is not to say there was anything dull about Helen's religion. On the contrary, she loved to express her new-found faith in joyful songs and celebrations. So she fitted in well with Charlie Wantage. Helen also reasoned that, since becoming a Christian was the greatest discovery in her life, she ought to share the secret with others. She readily accepted the invitation to become a Sunday School teacher and prepared the lessons with care and enthusiasn. Further, she began telling other women about her Christianity and initiated a small Bible study group which met weekly in her house. From her very limited income, she would put aside ten per cent each week to give away to others. When Bet and I considered how worried she had once been about having enough to live on, we marvelled at her new confidence that God would meet all her material needs. We felt humbled, too, by her readiness to make sacrifices as she worked out her Christian faith in daily living.

Helen's new-found beliefs had other consequences too. She drew upon them to calm her natural tendency to become agitated with her children and to shout at them. A more relaxed attitude in the home seemed to benefit both Julie and Francis. Helen continued to throw herself enthusiastically into her role as craft leader at the junior youth club. She planned the activities beforehand and many youngsters, especially the girls, left delighted with the model, picture, calendar or whatever, which Helen had taught them to make out of cardboard, paper and glue. Once I had felt drained by Helen's demands, now I felt cheered and encouraged by her support.

So, I was more than ready to act as a god-parent. Julie and Francis were well above the normal age for a christening but Charlie Wantage assured Helen that this did not matter. So one crisp, January Sunday afternoon we gathered around the font in St Matthew's. Along with a few relatives, Helen had invited Dylan and Doreen Willis, Ted and Roly Williams, Bet and myself.

Julie and Francis were usually fidgety, 'ants-in-the-pants' type children. Perhaps influenced by the solemnity of the occasion – or by the promise of christening presents waiting to be opened – they stood quietly and expectantly. Christening rituals can often be just a form of words. This time, Helen's new experience and her understanding of its spiritual significance made it a moving and sincere service. Although few in numbers, we sang the hymns with loud voice. We then knelt as the Rev. Wantage prayed God's blessing and protection on Julie and Francis and all children in Edgely.

After baptizing the children, Charlie spoke briefly about the importance of Christian families. Never one to skirt around a difficult subject, he spoke of the fact that the children he had just baptized had no father present at the church, that no husband was standing to share the vows with Helen. But, he continued, it was likely that Joseph had died when Jesus was young – so that Jesus too had spent most of his boyhood without an earthly father. Mary had raised her son in the paths of goodness without the support of a husband. Charlie expressed his confidence that with God's help Helen would succeed in her task of raising a happy family.

As Charlie preached his sermon, I looked out of the corner of my eye at Dylan and Doreen, at Ted and Roly and at Helen sitting with her children but no partner. They were

138

all families and all had something to contribute to making Edgely a better place for families. Helen caught my eye and smiled. We filed out into the cold, frosty air. Whatever the new year might bring, I thought, it could be faced with more confidence because of people like Helen. I gave thanks to God.

A few weeks later, I wasn't feeling like giving thanks to anybody. I was in court again.

The court usher greeted me as I pushed into the waiting-room.

'You again. I'd better issue you with a season ticket.'

'Don't bother,' I grinned. 'Just get a tea machine installed in this dog kennel.'

This time I was appearing with Drew Sprite. With little control from his weak parents, Drew was growing into an obnoxious teenager. His readiness to respond to any frustration with kicks from his boots made him feared in some quarters. Even worse was the violence of his tongue. While replacing a missing tile on the roof of our house, I had overheard Drew's obscene tongue in action.

Fiona Scott had wandered into the garden, where Drew was just about to knock on our door.

'What do you want, you old bag?' he challenged. 'Bob's not in.'

'Mind your own business,' replied Fiona.

'Suppose you're looking for Legs. We all know what you get from him. Bet you've got a bun in the oven already.'

Fiona reddened.

'Oh no, I haven't. Anyway, it's nothing to do with you. Why don't you get back to your glue sniffing? Glue is about the only friend you've got.'

The normally pacific Fiona added a few more choice comments about Drew's smelliness and large ears.

He responded with a stream of crudities, ending, 'Oh, go and rub yourself against a lamp-post. That's what you're doing when you push yourself all close against Legs when you're on his motor bike. You're a dirty cow, just like your mother.'

Unable to reply, Fiona turned on her heels and ran away. Twelve-year-old Drew had put seventeen-year-old Fiona to flight by the power of his words.

If his tongue didn't land him in trouble, his nicking was bound to. He laughingly boasted that he regularly went shoplifting but was never caught. Eventually, he was nailed. Even so, it was for a minor offence. The police probably would not have prosecuted if he had not made himself so unpopular with them. On seeing a copper in the distance, Drew would scream 'pigs', put up two fingers and run away. He bragged constantly about his greatest coup – when a police car had been parked outside Webster's house, Drew had opened the door and stolen some tools from it. The case of the missing ferret gave the police their turn.

Ferret-breeding was taken seriously in Edgely. Ferrets were used in the nearby hills in order to sniff out rabbits. Mr Finch liked his stewed rabbit and took pride in his ferrets. On discovering the theft of a young one from his shed, he sent for the police and voiced his suspicions about the loud-mouthed Drew. Police Constable Driver called on the Sprites and caught Drew with the ferret actually about his body. Even Drew could not talk his way out of that. Dickie Driver was a fair-minded bloke but Drew's tauntings had, as the boys put it, 'got up his nose'. With a more amenable youngster, he might have issued a warning. In the face of Drew's defiance, he wanted a prosecution.

So once again we stood in the courtroom. Once again we had a long wait, for courts seem unable to stagger appearances and make every case report at 10 a.m. Once again Joey Stackpoole had prepared a report on behalf of the Social Services Department. As Mr Sprite opted to stay at home to look after Jake, it was a worried and concerned Mrs Sprite to whom Joey was now talking. Rose Sprite was hard of hearing and Joey went carefully and slowly through her report. Drew expressed indifference. Shrugging his shoulders at Joey's attempts to involve him, he began to talk to the other offenders. His short gingery hair bristled like an angry cat. His small piggy eyes glistened, and he waggled his ears. He was making the most of the occasion, drawing as much attention to himself as he could.

For all his horrible ways, there was still something I liked about Drew. His chin jutted out in a defiance which was prepared to take on the whole world. His cheeky, crude humour was often hurtful but sometimes very funny. It was about to be seen in action again.

The usher approached and asked Mrs Sprite for her address. She failed to hear and he repeated himself in a louder voice. The unfortunate woman misunderstood.

'Undress. Undress? What for? I'm not going to undress here.' Drew was beside himself with laughter.

'Here mate,' he addressed the usher. 'Don't get her to undress. You might say she'd be "court" with her knickers down. "Court", get it?'

The other boys gathered round Drew in a sniggering circle. Again I observed his power to enlist people quickly on his side in order to humiliate others.

The usher then did his ushering. As we filed into the courtroom, he poked Drew and indicated that he would soon be laughing on the other side of his face.

The bench consisted of familiar faces, Mr Senior, Mr Garth and a lady whom I now knew to be Miss Wright, a headmistress. PC Driver rose to recite how he had been summoned by Mr Finch and directed to Drew. He continued, reading slowly from his notebook.

'I knocked at the boy's house in order to pursue my investigation. Drew Sprite answered the door and I observed a ferret snuggled within his jumper. I said that I had reason to believe that the ferret was the property of Mr Finch. The boy wriggled about a lot, admitted it was Mr Finch's and declared that the ferret had bitten his private parts.'

Mr Senior raised his eyebrows and interrupted.

'Are you sure that's what he said?'

'Not exactly, sir, he employed more colourful language which I thought it best to modify.'

'Constable, we are not in a ladies' seminary. Please stick to the facts.'

'Yes sir. The boy then unzipped his trousers, threw the

141

creature at me and suggested I stuffed it down Mr Finch'
throat. I took this to mean that he admitted it belonged to
the said Mr Finch. At this juncture, his mother returned and
angrily remonstrated with me for being present while her
son had his trousers down. I enlightened her as to the nature
of my call and she apologized. While she tended to her son'
injuries, I informed them what action would be taken and
that a statement would be required.'

Eventually, PC Driver concluded his case. Drew admitted
the offence. Joey, pushing aside her haystack blonde hair,
distributed her report. I read it through rapidly. Her short
account stated that Mr and Mrs Sprite failed to maintain
discipline but did love their son. She pointed out that, as I
was already closely associated with the family, there was little
point in involving the Social Services Department, at this
point. She recommended a fine. The magistrates whispered
together, then asked Mrs Sprite what she had to say.

Rose Sprite nervously stood up. She was dressed in a dark
suit, wore make-up and her gingery hair was neatly brushed.
An attractive face was ruined by lines of worry.

'I don't know what to say, your worship. He's a good boy
really. A bit wild. He's ever so good with Jake – our youngest. He loves animals, I think that's why he took the ferret.
Perhaps I should buy him one.'

She sat down and wiped her brow with a lace handkerchief.

Drew had nothing to say. Mr Senior gave him a lecture,
stressing that his school report was bad and that unless he
improved he would be in deep trouble. He imposed a modest
fine and recommended that Drew be made to pay from his
own pocket. Leaving the court, I heard Drew declaring
loudly, so that PC Driver would hear, that his mum would
pay the fine. The policeman, who considered the magistrates
much too lenient, brought his large face within an inch of
Drew's.

'I'll be looking for you, Sprite,' he snarled. 'And when I
nail you next time, you'll wish that ferret had finished you
off.'

I sighed. Unless Drew changed, he would finish up in
Borstal just like Phil Peters.

Dryden Borstal had released Phil Peters some time back. The demands of Webster, Blondie, Lorna, Flo and others meant that I had rarely visited him. I think Phil resented this, for he now kept his distance.

Mrs Peters was delighted to have Phil back, but his return coincided with another arrival. It had been Daphne Peters' Saturday night habit to enjoy some drinks and flirtations at 'Caesar's', a town centre night club. Here she met Ken Standen, a divorced man employed as a bus conductor, and eventually he moved in with her. Tall, slim and bearded, he was five years younger than Daphne, who was flattered by his attentions. Certainly, she made no secret of their relationship.

'You know me, Bob, I always enjoy a ride,' she winked at me. 'Isn't he gorgeous? You see, you've missed your chance.'

That did not bother me! I was worried what effect Ken's arrival would have on the Peters boys. Jardine had already tried to take on the role of the top man in the home and had spent a couple of nights at our house following a row with mum. To my amazement, Ken's arrival created few initial problems. A cheerful and extrovert man, he made an effort to win the approval of the boys. Danny, now four years old, and already subject to taunts about the colour of his skin, badly needed the attention of a man. Ken was prepared to play with him. Jardine and ten-year-old Troy appreciated both the free bus rides Ken provided and the faster trips in his old Cortina. Moreover, Mrs Peters began to look after the inside of the home as carefully as she did her appearance. So things improved all round.

By contrast, Phil's long-anticipated return seemed to stir up trouble. For a start it meant re-shuffling the sleeping arrangements so that he could have a bedroom. Danny was moved to a mattress alongside Mrs Peters and Ken. As Danny tended to wake at the slightest movement, the couple began to feel deprived. Daphne, never one to suffer in silence, complained to her friends that for years her 'urgings' had been neglected and now – having found a virile lover – they could hardly move without Danny bawling his head off.

Jardine no longer had a room to himself, for he had to share with Troy. Rather unfairly, he blamed Phil. Not least, a rivalry developed between Ken and Phil as to who was the number one male in the house.

The overcrowding and tensions might have been less stressful if Jardine and Phil had found regular jobs. Jardine left school at a time of rising unemployment. He wanted to be a garage mechanic – as did 500 other school leavers. Phil, with his muscular strength, did secure two labouring jobs. Unfortunately, his clumsiness and inability to listen to instructions soon brought him into conflict with foremen. He lost the first job when, contrary to instructions, he started a cement mixer whose handle flew off and landed in a nearby greenhouse. The second job seemed more suited to his disposition – it was with a demolition company! Again, he did not listen. Armed with a sledgehammer, he smashed everything in sight, including some valuable wooden doors which the firm wished to retain for sale. Sacked again.

Phil's enforced inactivity brought him back into contact with me. Bored and unhappy at home, he began to drop in for cups of coffee. Jardine was eventually fixed up with a government-sponsored job in a butcher's shop, while I engaged Phil in a search for work. We followed up advertisements and knocked at factories. We failed, but our joint efforts drew us together in friendship. We began to talk about his rivalry with Ken and his resentment with mum for bringing a fancy man home just as he was released from Borstal.

Phil tended to spend his dole money at 'Caesar's'. The club provided booze, strip-tease and dancing. Rumour was that drugs were pedalled there. Phil liked to give the image of a hard-drinking type with money to flash around. 'Caesar's' was one place where his Borstal record and readiness to use his fists brought forth admiration from a bevy of girls.

Eventually, he fell for Lucy Wall. Petite, with big eyes, full breasts and dyed blonde hair, Lucy specialized in slit skirts and see-through blouses. Phil thought she was wonderful and brought her to meet me. Certainly, she was

144

attractive, but a hardness about her lips made me feel uneasy. Worse, Lucy began to draw Phil into a criminal fraternity. She came from a neighbouring town where her father and brothers had a reputation as small-time racketeers in the secondhand car trade. Phil began to spend time there. His strength came in useful when engines had to be lifted and dents banged out. His reward was freedom to drive the cars. Phil's wheel spins and hard braking soon became a familiar sound on the Edgely's roads.

During the Autumn, a friend offered Charlie Wantage an off-peak camping holiday in the Lake District. Unable to go himself, the vicar passed it on to me. So in the school half-term, I took a small party to Keswick. Dylan, who was becoming my closest friend, took some time off work and squeezed Doreen, Rebecca, Phil and Jardine into his dad's car. I drove the mini-van accompanied by Bet, Drew and most of the gear. Webster was desperate to come but his boss ruled that he was not yet due for a holiday.

We pitched the tents close to the shimmering Lake Derwentwater. It looked inviting but was icy cold – as Drew discovered when he dived in and even more quickly jumped out. Light rain in the first few days did not deter us from walking and climbing the hills and peaks. The falling, yellow leaves made a golden carpet beneath our feet. Drew, Jardine and Rebecca were continually throwing handfuls of the leaves at us and hauling themselves up trees.

Phil spent much of his time wrestling with Dylan. Despite Phil's brawn, it was usually Dylan who won – a fact which drew Phil's grudging respect. Indeed, Dylan was a gem. His athletic prowess was admired by the boys, yet he never bossed them about. He took his turn in organizing the camp, seeing that the chores were completed and the youngsters kept quiet at night.

Jardine enjoyed the company of Bet and Doreen. Like Webster, he considered himself adept at chatting up the ladies and he even volunteered to peel the spuds. His attachment left me free to concentrate on Drew. He needed it, for he possessed an inbuilt radar system which led him to trouble. If aggressive lads were around, Drew was sure to confront them. If he walked into a shop, he invariably aroused the suspicions of the shopkeeper. If he entered a café his habit of snapping plastic spoons, smearing brown sauce around and his loud remarks would lead to rebuffs from customers and staff.

Phil was prepared to help with Drew. I had been worried about their relationship, for Drew tended to glorify Phil as the tough, hard-bittened criminal. To his credit, Phil constantly warned him about the folly of crime. During one walk, Drew felt thirsty and nicked a couple of bottles of milk from a doorstep. It was Phil who made him return them, giving a lecture on how small crimes led to big ones. I expressed my gratitude and Phil glowed with pleasure.

Within the camp, Phil was ready to do his share of cooking, washing up and re-pitching the tent after Drew loosened the tent pegs. He was also willing to contribute cash. He treated us to meals and took us to the cinema. He bought prayer books for Bet and Doreen as a 'thank you' for their cooking. But where did the money come from? He was still on the dole and much of this he gave to Mrs Peters. I was reluctant to probe into his affairs for fear of offending him.

Then one morning we had a long chat over a coffee in the Wimpy Bar while the others were shopping in Woolworth's. The rain, beating against the windows, made us feel dry, warm and close as we sipped our drink. Phil opened up, talking about his liking for young Drew and how it made him feel better when he helped him. He declared his love for Lucy – he had phoned her every day – and his intention of marrying her. Gently, I voiced my worries about the money he was flashing around.

Phil frowned for a moment, then reassured me.

'Don't worry, Bob. Lucy's brothers pay me for the work I do on their cars. The social security people don't know and you won't grass me. I won't do anything that would get me sent back inside, I couldn't stand that. I want to get my own place, settle down with Lucy. Don't worry.'

Soon after, I had more immediate worries. The rain became torrential. Half-way through the night, we found our

146

camp beds surrounded by two inches of water. The field had become an extension of Lake Derwentwater. There was no option save to stuff the gear into the mini-van and to sit in the vehicles. At dawn we drove off and enjoyed a fried, greasy breakfast in a transport café.

The rain continued to pour down, so we drove to Carlisle and spent the evening in the cinema. An uncomfortable night was passed as we attempted to sleep in the vehicles. Drew was able to curl up in the back of the mini-van. Bet and I huddled together, although the gear-stick and handbrake tended to come between us. Next morning we drove home by way of the motorway. The trip took all day, for the boys insisted on stopping at every motorway café in order to play the machines.

That evening, tired and wet, we chugged into Edgely. The youngsters declared it a great holiday.

Following the holiday, Phil devoted much of his time to being with Lucy. But he still liked to associate with his Edgely friends and was particularly keen to participate in our first football matches. Using the Blackway pitch – with its open air dressing-rooms – I had arranged a number of games against clubs from other parts of the town.

I played in goal. Webster Summerfield and Syd Battle had never been able to get into their school teams, yet they developed as a pair of reliable backs. Dylan was the nominal centre back, although his energy took him all over the field. He would boot a goal kick, rush up to take the resulting throw-in and the next moment emerge to place the ball for a corner. Jardine, Phil and Don Plumb made up the mid-field.

Jardine's talent and enthusiasm was somewhat spoilt by a tendency to lose heart too easily. Phil contributed crunching tackles and mule-like kicks. Don was too fat to make a footballer, yet he often managed to place his bulk in the right place at the right ime.

Up front, the speedy Legs Lancing, Drew Sprite and Mac Scott loved to score goals, followed by TV-style gestures to the screaming bevy of girls who came to support us. Lastly,

Fangs Battle also turned out. He didn't know much about football but his ferocious expressions sometimes scared the opposition.

Residents of Edgely began to take an interest in its first football team. Mrs Battle and Mrs Plumb organized a jumble sale and purchased football shirts with the profits. Red Moore pinned the teams and the results in the shop window. Phil contributed his enthusiasm. During the kick-about practices on the hill, he suggested moves to be tried in the games. There was only one drawback – his temper. He so hated losing that, if the scores were going against us, he would start to blame the referee or to pick trouble with the other team.

The tension came to a head in one match when, after being heavily barged, he hit an opposing player so hard he knocked him out. Drew Sprite, ever ready for trouble, rushed to put the boot in, while Webster began shouting that the referee had been bribed. Eventually, the referee, Dylan and myself restored order. Phil was sent off. Later I put it straight to Phil – he had to control his temper or miss some matches.

To his credit, Phil accepted my warning and continued to back the Edgely project. The northern, more affluent side of the town possessed a pitch-and-putt golf course. Most of our club members had not played, so Dylan, Phil and I took them over to introduce them to the ancient sport. The experiment almost failed to start. Jardine, who had purchased Webster's moped, drove his machine up the fairway, skidded around the green and uprooted the flagpole. An enraged official wanted to kick us all out and I mollified him only by ordering Jardine home. He roared off in anger, shouting that he didn't want to play golf which was a game for pouffs like me.

The next problem was that Drew was in one of his look-for-trouble moods. His idea of golf was to wait for no one. He drove his ball, ran, smote it again and so on. He barged into other players on the course and played right through their games. At this point, Phil proved his worth. He warned Drew that if he got us chucked out, he would hit him so hard that his teeth would stick out of the back of his neck.

Having frightened him, he then proceeded to play alongside Drew. Thereafter, the game proceeded smoothly, and some of the teenagers enjoyed themselves so much that we determined to hold a club golf competition.

Phil gained status and satisfaction from his involvement. It also continued to draw us close to each other. Yet I still felt uneasy. He drove a vast array of cars and was never short of money. I sensed two Phils. One was an enthusiastic supporter of our project, an apparently reformed delinquent who warned other lads of the dire consequences of taking up crime. The other was an increasingly sophisticated con-man who was being drawn into an adult criminal network.

At Christmas time, Phil had a scrape with the police. Lucy wanted a Christmas tree, so Phil determined to obtain a large one. The best tree was sited outside a fashionable church on the posh side of town. One evening, Phil removed the tree, quickly shoved it into his car and drove off. Unfortunately for him, he overlooked the fact that the coloured lights which decorated the tree were still plugged in. The wires became entangled, and tree, car and Phil were dragged to a halt. At this moment, a police car arrived. Both police and magistrates must have seen the funny side, for Phil escaped with a small fine.

One month later Phil and Lucy married. She was pregnant. They secured a flat in a large Edwardian house in Lucy's town. Mrs Peters was upset. Not so much because Phil had been sleeping with his girl as because he gave her just two days' notice of the registry office wedding. He did not invite me. Nonetheless, Bet and I stood outside the door and took a few snaps as they emerged.

Phil wore a light blue suit and waistcoat. Lucy looked minute beside him but most male eyes were on her small frame. Despite the wintry weather, she wore a short, flowered dress and a pill-box hat. Her four brothers, looking like broad-shouldered members of the mafia, were busy stacking crates of beer into their large cars.

Thereafter, Phil rarely came to Edgely. Living in Lucy's neighbourhood, his days as well as his nights were spent with her family. At least Phil's move relieved some of the overcrowding in the Peters household and the tensions lessened.

Within a month of being married, Phil was arrested and taken into custody. Worse, he resisted arrest, injured a policeman with a chair, and was taken only when reinforcements were summoned. At his trial, it emerged that he and the Wall brothers had been engaged in an extensive car racket. They had specialized in stealing tyres, wheels, car radios and engine parts which were then sold to shady spare dealers. A few cars had also been taken, resprayed and sold on the secondhand market. My fears were justified. Phil had been leading a double life. And to think that with some of his ill-gotten gains he had bought prayer books for Bet and Doreen.

The brothers, the ringleaders, were sentenced to three years in prison. Phil's longer stretch of five years was imposed, it seemed, partly because he had a previous record and partly because he was the only member of the gang to resort to violence. The local paper splashed the trial on the front page, giving prominence to the judge's remarks that thugs who wounded policemen could expect no mercy from him.

A heartbroken Daphne Peters had to witness her son follow his father to jail. She declared she wanted nothing more to do with him. She even seemed to blame me for failing to turn her quick-tempered, delinquent son into a stable law-abiding citizen. I wanted to retort that Phil had felt rejected on finding a new man in the bed once occupied by his dad. But to have spoken in anger would have achieved nothing. I kept quiet and accepted her sneer that Phil had successfully pulled the wool over my eyes.

At the trial, Lucy, whose pregnancy was obvious, wept and screamed that she would wait for her husband. Jardine was in despair, for he had been growing nearer to his brother. One person did enjoy the case. Drew Sprite was electrified by the knowledge that his friend had broken the arm of one policeman and almost defeated the efforts of four others to hold him down. He boasted that he and Phil would become

150

partners after his release from prison. He cut out the newspaper reports, tried to talk like Phil and even imitated his swaggering walk. If Phil had wanted to influence Drew, he had certainly succeeded – in the wrong direction.

In the Spring, Lucy gave birth to baby Greta. I typed a letter to the prison governor, asking permission to take Lucy and the baby to visit Phil. The prison welfare officer replied stating that inmates could receive one visit a month after they had settled in, but that 220436 Peters, was still being 'routinized', so that a visit would require special permission granted only in exceptional circumstances – and would I always cite the prisoner's number. I wrote again, emphasizing that 220436 Peters had never seen his child. Eventually I phoned and the welfare officer reluctantly agreed to go to the great administrative inconvenience of sending a pass.

I had hoped Daphne Peters would accompany us. She refused. So, on a Spring morning, Lucy and I set off with Greta gurgling away in a carrycot in the back of the minivan. The prison was a modern one, located miles from anywhere in the Midlands countryside. On arrival, I searched vainly for a handle on the huge glass door. I jumped a foot in the air when a voice said:

'Don't smear the glass, what do you want?'

I spoke into a grid and waved the pass. After a long pause – presumably while a special beam searched me for a machine-gun – the glass panel slid open. We walked inside and waited. Waiting, inside large institutions, seems to be rule No. 1. We waited until instructed to walk along a glass tunnel. Lucy stopped to brush her hair and pull up her stockings. A warder, perched on a desk, checked our names against the list and jerked his thumb to indicate that we could move forward and wait with other visitors in a large room.

The room contained a number of tables, a canteen and, I was pleased to see, a play area with toys for children. The prisoners began to appear through a door at the far end. A warder directed them to tables, and parents, wives and children joined them for a brief visit.

Phil was one of the last to walk through. He had lost

weight, looked strained, but still displayed his old swagger. Phil made straight for Greta, picked her up, kissed her, held her above his head.

'She's lovely, she's beautiful, she's mine.'

Then he turned to Lucy and embraced her.

'Cor, I am missing you. Takes a gallon of bromide to keep me calm. You're not playing around with anyone else are you? I think about that. A lot of the blokes in here lose their women.'

'No, love,' Lucy replied soothingly. 'I am waiting for you. Mind you, it's hard with so little money. What with the boys and you inside, I have to rely on dad slipping me a bit. Social security is not enough.'

'Sorry love. I will make it up to you when I get out.'

Phil held Lucy with one hand and examined Greta's little fingers with the other.

'Where's mum, Bob? She hasn't written to me.'

I hesitated.

'She's taken it hard, Phil. You write to her and I think she will come round.'

Phil talked about prison life. Conditions were good, food was all right and the cells were not overcrowded. The problem was that prisoners spent much of the time locked in their cells. Phil felt like a caged bird. He spoke wistfully of the wide-open spaces at Keswick.

'Sometimes I feel as though I am going to burst. I am surrounded by walls. The only noise is the rattle of keys. I could escape, you know. I could get over the walls.'

'Don't be mad, Phil,' snapped Lucy. 'You'd be caught, get a longer sentence and the screws would give you hell. It's bad enough waiting five years.'

Phil, near to tears, nursed Greta. While Lucy went to buy some cigarettes he asked about his brothers and Drew. He urged me to tell Drew not to follow in his footsteps.

I think a lot about what we did together, Bob. Remember those football matches? I know I let you down, but when I come out I want to help you. I am making something for you and Bet – a caravan. Not a real one, you wally. A

152

matchstick one. Doing these models keeps me from cracking up.'

Lucy returned and I went to the canteen, to leave them alone. As I sat down, a man wearing a clerical collar approached me.

'Mr Laken? I guessed it was you talking to Peters. I'm Menzies, the chaplain. I've seen a good deal of Phil and you obviously mean a lot to him. How did he seem?'

I shook his hand.

'Very shaken. He can't stand being restricted. Borstal was bad enough and there he was working in the garden. Still, he is meeting his daughter today.'

Richard Menzies shook his head as he lit his pipe. He was in his late fifties with grey, receding hair. A large, bear-like man, he must have made a good father-figure to the prisoners.

'He's making life very difficult for himself,' he continued. 'The reason he spends so much time in his cell is that he is so abusive to the staff. He threw a plate at one recently and cut his head. When his case comes before the governor he'll lose more privileges, probably have family visits banned for a time.'

'That's ridiculous,' I protested. 'Visits are only once a month anyway. He just lives to see Lucy and Greta. Banning visits will make him worse.'

'My sentiments exactly,' he agreed. 'That's why I want you to hammer into Phil's thick skull that his aggressive behaviour only harms himself and his family. Listen, if family visits are banned, it will be important that you still come. I can probably get you in on a professional pass – that's for people like probation officers. Approach me, not the welfare officer for that.'

Thanking him, I returned to Phil and began to urge him to conform to the rules. A buzzer went. A recorded voice told all visitors to leave. Phil hugged Lucy and kissed little Greta. He shouted a request that I send him a photo of Greta and some matchsticks. Fathers were reluctantly letting go of their children. Wardens were separating husbands from wives. If they could obtain transport and passes, they might

153

see each other briefly in a month's time. I did not envy Richard Menzies his job.

Phil was punished by losing visits for three months. My letter to the governor, requesting permission to send him matchsticks, met the curt reply that prison supplies were quite adequate. I drove over to inform Lucy of his loss of privileges. Her reaction surprised me. She shrugged her shoulders.

'He's a fool,' she said. 'He'll lose his remission. And he expects me to wait five years. Five years sitting at home with a kid. He seems to forget I'm a woman.'

Looking at Lucy in a mini-skirt and tight jumper, I didn't think anyone could forget she was a woman. She stood up, applied some lipstick and looked approvingly at herself in the mirror. She lifted the passive Greta into the pram.

'My mum's looking after Greta for a bit. I'm going to the club. Look, Bob, I like a drink and a bit of male company. You tell Phil I'm waiting for him. That'll keep him happy. When I can I'll take Greta to see him. But I might have a bit on the side and there's no reason why he should know.'

I left, feeling that I had gone through the same sad predicament with Flo Scott. I sympathized with Lucy but dreaded to imagine the effect on Phil if she was unfaithful to him.

Shortly afterward, I received a phone call from Richard Menzies. The next day he sent a special pass and this time I drove alone to the prison. Once through the glass door, I was led to Richard's office. The warder was sent to collect Phil.

'Thanks for coming, Bob. It's hard to explain what has happened to Phil, so I wanted him to tell you.'

Phil was brought in. He relaxed on seeing me and asked after his wife and child. While we talked, Richard made some coffee and handed Phil a fag. Then Phil recounted his experience.

'Just over a week ago, I was stretched out on my bunk when a light came into the cell. I can't describe it, the place kind of shone. Anyway, I guessed it was God. I stood up, felt funny and knelt down. All I could say was the Lord's Prayer. Then the horrible things I've done pressed down on

154

me. I prayed and it was like a weight lifted off me. Then the light went. I felt great, I was crying. I told my mates when they returned. They laughed and said I was a nutter. But Mr Menzies believed me and I knew you'd understand, Bob.'

I did understand and expressed my delight. Soon after, Phil was taken back to his cell.

'It's a long way to bring you for such a short meeting,' Richard Menzies commented. 'But I wanted you to hear for yourself. I'm not sure what to make of it. Prisoners sometimes profess a conversion in order to win attention from me, or as a means of getting a cushy job. The screws think Phil is trying to con me. Yet his story has a ring of truth about it. I know we can count on your prayers.'

I sat in the mini outside the prison. Light rain was falling. I undid the thermos flask and swilled my cheese sandwiches down with tea. Beyond those walls was Phil. The screws and perhaps the other prisoners would give him a hard time. His mum was refusing to write. Lucy's behaviour might cause him deep pain. I hoped his spiritual experience was a true one, for he would need something to enable him to survive the succeeding years.

9

The Skies Crash Down

The Edgely Project was due to finish in September. The energetic Charlie Wantage had persuaded the Community Christian Council to extend the date until the end of November. Following this, he set about writing a report to convince the CCC that I should be funded for a further three years.

Charlie's confidence was a source of encouragement. I was also pleased with the youth clubs. They possessed a stability which sprang from a regular membership and the involvement of several parents. Further, PC Dickie Driver had started to drop in to the clubs. Despite his private war with Drew Sprite, Dickie was keen to relate to the teenagers. As he played darts, let them try on his helmet, answered innumerable questions about crime, a greater trust and respect developed between him and the members.

Bet, too, was happy. As an infant school teacher and part of the Project, she became a well-known figure. When she walked down the road, nearly every person smiled a greeting and small children often rushed to win her attention. Then she had an accident which was the fore-runner of a series of disasters so severe as to make me want to pack up.

Our roof had leaks which channelled water through the ceiling into the bedroom. That summer was marked by heavy rain. I placed bowls in the loft to prevent the drips entering our room. Returning home one Saturday, I heard Bet up in the loft trying to empty the bowls. I climbed the stairs and shouted to her to leave the job to me. Too late. She slipped off a rafter, crashed through the plaster and landed on the bedroom floor. She was in pain and I phoned for an ambulance. A broken wrist, severe bruising and shock ment a stay in hospital.

On the Monday, I visited Bet in hospital. By now she was able to laugh, speculating what would have happened if she had landed on top of me. Returning home, I picked up a note from Dylan and Doreen asking me round for supper after club. Remembering club, I went upstairs to sort out some change for the café.

Instead of banking entrance fees and café profits, I had been storing them in a locked cupboard in the spare bedroom. My heart plunged. The cupboard door had been smashed, the cash had gone.

Checking doors and windows, I deduced that no one had broken into the house. My suspicions concentrated on Webster Summerfield. Some time before, our spare door key had gone missing. Webster, a frequent visitor, would have had ample chance to lift it. Moreover, he knew where the café money was kept. Webster. I could have wept.

After he obtained the part-time job at the Richmond Hotel things had gone smoothly. Apart from occasional temper outbursts, he had worked hard and was taken on as a full-time kitchen assistant. The long hours, often involving evening work, filled his time. His earnings meant he had cash in his pocket. He invested in a secondhand moped and later in a motor bike. The following summer his one-year supervision order was completed without a hitch.

Soon after, the cracks appeared. Most devastating, he lost his job. Following several tiffs with colleagues over what Saturdays he could have off, Webster had participated in a fight, using eggs as ammunition. Mr Sellick somewhat displeased that the machine-gunning with eggs occurred in front of customers, sacked the kitchen staff.

Unemployment had two unfortunate results. Webster fell behind on his motor-bike hire purchase payments. He had time on his hands and was bored. He reverted to calling regularly at our home and continued to run the café at club. When he had sufficient petrol money, he rode into town and I wondered if he was shoplifting again. Then came the theft from our house.

I walked slowly up to Mrs Summerfield. I wondered if she

would angrily accuse me of picking on her son. Far from it. After I explained the facts, her heavy face scowled.

'That sounds like Webster all right. I'll get the truth, even if I beat him all night. The ungrateful toad. After all you and Bet have done for him. Flint, find your brother.'

The large, shambling Flint – also home on the dole – hastened to obey. Through the window, I saw him spreading the news. Webster had never been popular and was in for a rough time if he had nicked the youth club's money. Within a few minutes, Webster marched boldly through the door.

'Yes, what is it?'

'You know what. Where's the money you've nicked from Bob?'

'Honest, I don't know what you're talking about.'

Sandra, with swift movements, went through Webster's pockets. No money – but she fished out the key. He reluctantly admitted that he had picked up the key, yet still angrily denied the crime. His mum removed the leather belt that surrounded her ample girth. She jerked her thumb, and Webster bent over the back of an armchair. She commenced to lay the belt about him. I was amazed that a teenage boy should submit to the indignity. Such was Sandra's authority over her lads. After two or three strokes, she asked Webster to admit the theft. He shook his head, and the beating continued. Flint drew me aside, smashing one fist into another.

'Bob, just give me five minutes alone with him. I'll get it out of him with these fists.'

'I shook my head. The belting was upsetting me more than losing the money. Webster's long brown hair had fallen over his face. After each blow, he jerked in pain, so that the tossing hair revealed his crooked nose. Enough. I stepped between boy and belt.

'No more, Sandra. Let me talk to him outside.'

'All right, but don't go soft on him,' she panted.

At the front gate, I looked straight at him.

'Webster, we've been through so much together. Don't spoil it now. Tell me the truth and we'll find some way you can repay the money.

He would not meet my gaze. He turned away and walked down the road.

Back home, I sat miserably drinking a coffee. A knock. Through the door pane, I could see Webster's silhouette. He slouched in.

'Here's the money. I've spent five pounds. What are you going to do about it?'

The following day, Tuesday, I awoke still feeling sick with disappointment about Webster. At the hospital, I determined to say nothing, but Bet saw that I was down and extracted the truth from me. Still, we were cheered by the news that she would be allowed home the next day.

Returning at lunch-time, I met Mac Scott with a note from his mum asking me to call, 'urgent'.

I had seen little of Flo Scott and Ritchie Crosby over the past year. They had not even come on the Project outing. Ritchie worked long hours and frequented the pub. Apart from her visits to old Mr Blenkinsop, Flo stayed mainly in the house, content with her domestic tasks. Occasionally, we met in the street. She never invited me in and obviously felt she could cope without my help. Sometimes, I ruefully considered that Flo's potential for talking about political issues or for educating herself were being neglected. Still, as she told me, she was happy with her man and children.

Of course, I had frequent contact with the latter. Fiona, now seventeen, was working in a school kitchen, Mac who was broadening out physically, had settled down at school where he shone at all sports. Ishbael remained quiet, demure and polite. Fiona and Mac were regulars at the youth club, where our friendship was such that they knew they could always turn to me for a chat.

Mac pushed open the front door. The room had the same scrubbed, too-tidy, appearance. Not a toy, newspaper or book in sight. Mac shouted and Flo descended the stairs. She had put on weight and a few grey hairs were noticeable amongst the black. For once, her hair looked uncombed. Her dark eyes bore the signs of a sleepless night. She motioned with her hand and Mac disappeared.

Flo turned her back and looked out of the window.

'I'm finished, Bob. He's walked out on me. We're up to our necks in debt. The electricity is to be cut off. The cruelty man is taking me to court. The kids will be put in a Home. So they should. I can't handle them.'

She faced me. The sun glinting through the window made it difficult for my eyes to focus on her. Nevertheless, I could see the tears streaming down her face. Moving to the side-board, she handed me the final demand from the Electricity Board.

Telling Flo to sit down, I made some coffee. She sank into an armchair and in a dull, lifeless voice brought me up to date. Ritchie had been laid off work. Bored, he began to spend lunch-hours at his pub. Social security meant less income, while he was spending more on booze. They argued over money. Ritchie complained that Flo no longer wanted to accompany him to the pub. She retorted that she liked dancing not drinking and that anyway they could not afford to go out. Flo had maintained the rent, but the coal and electricity bills were in arrears. Further, she believed she was pregnant. She had wanted so much to have a child by Ritchie. Now she could not bring herself to tell him.

Finally, the day before, they had had a tremendous row. Flo heard that Ritchie had had his arm around a woman at the pub. In anger, she accused him of carrying-on instead of searching for a job. He replied that she was in love with the duster not him and that she could take herself and the kids back to their real dads. Ritchie then packed a bag and stormed out. When he did not return, a distraught Flo went to look for him. Mac and Fiona were at the youth club, so she left Ishbael alone. Someone phoned the NSPCC to report that Flo was leaving a young child alone and to accuse her of beating the others with a stick.

Tuesday morning, Ritchie had still not reappeared. Instead, the NSPCC Inspector had called.

'Oh, Bob, it sounded so bad. I had to admit that I left her and that I do cane them. He asked me who their fathers were. I felt like some monster. Ritchie's not back. Suppose he's gone with that pub woman. I can't pay the bills. I want to give up.'

Bet came home from the hospital on the Wednesday. Despite the worries about Webster and Flo, I decided to spend the day at home. I settled Bet in the armchair, waved away her protests about not being an invalid, and prepared lunch.

We had just enjoyed omelette and chips when Jules Thomas arrived. His face was almost grey, his large lips trembled.

'Jules, what is it?'

'The baby's dead.'

Lorna had developed a routine for looking after Elvis and Clint. Bernard or Jules would wake her up in the morning. She washed and fed the babies and prepared a midday meal. In the afternoon, Mrs Plumb and Toni Hale took it in turns to keep an eye on them while Lorna did household jobs or escaped into town. In the evening, Becky Thomas was prepared to lend a hand. The extra help was needed for whereas Elvis was a strong, healthy lad, Clint was sickly and restless. The Health Visitor and Dr Keen frequently called.

On that fateful Wednesday, Lorna had put Clint in his cot for a morning nap. He was usually a fitful sleeper and noting that he was not stirring, Lorna investigated. Clint was face down on the mattress – dead. Lorna screamed and screamed. Bernard sent Jules to phone the hospital. An ambulance rushed small Clint away but it was too late.

When I arrived, Lorna was weeping hysterically, 'What did I do wrong? Did I kill him?'

Becky had rushed from her bookshop and sat cuddling her bereaved teenage daughter. Bernard was nursing Elvis. Ron Keen was summoned and tried to explain that it was a cot death.

For once our young GP made a wrong diagnosis. A post-mortem and inquest established that Clint died from a virus. The coroner emphasized that no blame attached to the mother; the virus was so powerful that death would probably have resulted, even if Clint had been in hospital.

At Lorna's request, the funeral was held at Ebenezer. As I entered the small chapel, I saw the coffin already at the front. I had never seen such a small coffin. My spirits sank. When we had come to Edgely nearly three years before, the occupant of that wooden box had not been been born. Now his brief life was over.

Standing next to the coffin was the square-shouldered, reassuring figure of Ted Williams.

Little Miss Bird squeezed away at the organ and the service commenced.

Lorna, bowed and shaking, could hardly mouth the words of the hymn. Becky Thomas was on her right and Bernard – in the black suit he had bought for Elvis's dedication – on her left. Jules stood erect, his eyes continually darting towards his sister. The death had dissolved any hostility and drawn them closer together than ever before.

Stirling Drift did not appear. He was still seeking fame and fortune in Newcastle. I was relieved at his absence, for I had feared he would return in order to accuse Lorna of negligence.

Roly Williams, Mrs Plumb and Bet were the only invited mourners. Toni was looking after Elvis. The chapel was covered in flowers, all sent by the people of Edgely. In the gloom, the bright colours of the flowers symbolized the concern of our council estate.

Ted took the service with simplicity and sensitivity. He spoke about the way Lorna had coped so well. He emphasized that death was not the end of life. He spoke about the Christ who had conquered death.

We rose to leave. Even in despair and grief, Lorna looked beautiful. Her fair hair contrasted with her black clothes. I took her hands. She pushed her head into my jacket.

'Why Bob? Why did it have to happen?'

I had no answer.

Thursday evening of that eventful week, Bet sat eating fish fingers with her left hand as she watched the TV local news.

'Listen, Bob,' she hissed.

'We now have further details about the car accident on the

trunk road,' the newsreader intoned. 'The driver has been named as Mr Jock Bell and his companion Mrs Lucy Peters. Mr Bell and Mrs Peters were cut free by firemen and neither sustained serious injury. Mrs Peters' baby girl was thrown on to the road and sustained injuries which proved fatal . . . Farmers in the west are fearful that the heavy rain will cut profits . . .'

I switched off the TV. Bet put down her plate and took my hand.

'Oh, Bob. What about Phil?'

What about Phil? Since his spiritual experience, I had visited only once. But we exchanged regular letters in which I gave all the news about Edgely and as much as I could about his wife and child. Lucy had sent short letters – and now that Phil could receive family visits again – had asked me to drive her to the prison. The prison chaplain informed me that although Phil was still subject to temper outbursts, he was trying hard to control them and had started to attend services in the chapel. Further, Phil had been promised a job on the prison farm if his improvement continued.

Lucy had continued to frequent 'Caesar's'. Here she commenced an affair with Jock Bell, an articulate whisky-drinking Glaswegian car salesman. Judging by the cut of his suits, he was successful at his job. When I had visited Lucy, she tried to reassure me.

'Forget about it, Bob. It's not serious. He's got a wife and kids up north. I've a bloke in prison. He's willing to spend money on me. He makes me laugh, gives me a good time. Look, I'm not educated like you, there's not much I can do. All I've got is my looks and my love-making. And that's one thing I'm tops at. So it suits us both. Don't you spoil it by telling Phil. I'm not going to stay at home all the time and if Phil finds out he'll go to pieces.'

Lucy was right. I could do nothing.

Then came the tragedy. Jock and Lucy were driving to the seaside for the weekend when Jock, trying to impress with his driving, took a bend too fast and turned the car over. Wearing seat belts, the couple were protected from serious injury. Poor Greta was thrown right out of the car window. She died the day after Clint.

Richard Menzies broke the news of Greta to Phil. Apparently he said little, just sank deeper and deeper into a silent, brooding, depression. Richard told him nothing about the other man.

Greta was buried quickly and quietly, with only Lucy's family in attendance. Soon afterwards, I called at the flat. Making light of her bruises, Lucy came to the point about Phil.

'Look Bob,' she started, 'Phil and I should never have got married. I know now that I don't want to be tied down. Greta was all that held us together and now she's gone. I don't want to live with Jock, I want to see a bit of life before I settle down and have kids.'

I listened, thinking of Phil. I had come feeling sympathy for Lucy, expecting her to be grieving the loss of her baby. Instead, those hard lips were pouring out words that spoke only of herself.

'All right, I'm not a holy Joe like you,' she snapped, as though reading my thoughts. 'You want everyone to be good. You thought you could make Phil go straight. You're a fool. He's a villain, always will be. I'll tell you something. After playing football with your kids on Saturday afternoons, he would spend the night at 'Caesar's' picking up tarts and drinking himself silly. You haven't got the sense to see what's happening right in front of your face. Now you're worried that his tender feelings will be hurt because I'm through with him. Well, I'll tell him straight.'

Lucy kept her word. On the next visiting day, Jock drove her to the prison. When I offered to accompany her, she told me to get stuffed. I phoned Richard Menzies to forewarn him. Later he told me that within two minutes of sitting down Lucy told Phil about Jock and said she was not prepared to wait five years. Phil snapped, went berserk. Grabbing Lucy by the neck, he tried to throttle her. A horde of wardens were required to overcome him and later he could be calmed only by medical sedation. Lucy left and started divorce proceedings.

So much was happening at Edgely that I could not visit straight away. Then I went, accompanied by Dylan. The very sight of Phil was a shock. He shuffled in like a bent old man. His cheeks were hollow, his face lined. As he spoke, his hands shook and his eyes watered. Only a year before, the same Phil had chased around the Lake District hills, a picture of health and youth. He found it difficult to talk.

The words that did come out were words of vengeance and bitterness. He wanted revenge against Lucy, her family, her lover. He was bitter about prison, religion, life. He dismissed the screws as animals, the chaplain as a hypocrite. I guessed he spoke about us in the same vein. Yet he grasped our hands. I looked at his hands and recalled that once they had held a wife and daughter. Now, along with his freedom, he had lost them.

Friday. I was planning my day, sharing it between Webster, Lorna, Flo and Phil. Bet answered the phone. A worried frown crossed her bruised face.

'It's for you. Blondie. Sounds in a state.'

I took the receiver.

'I can't go on,' Blondie sobbed. 'He's taken all the money. He threatens to slash my face if I try to make him leave. Bob, you're got to help me.'

When Butter Martin had moved in towards the end of the previous year, Blondie had entered an elated high. Over six foot tall, Butter made a striking figure with his jet-black hair, leather cowboy jacket, tight blue jeans, and motor bike gloves. I laughed and pointed out that the leather was imitation and that he looked like a motor cyclist who'd lost his machine. Perhaps I was jealous. Blondie gloried in his reputation as a hard man. She loved to walk beside him as he paraded down the street. She enjoyed the whispers about his fighting abilities and the fear it inspired in some men. She saw the envy in the eyes of other young women.

I had continued to call. If Butter was out or still in bed, Blondie would recount their latest adventures. Butter's violence had already resulted in bans from two pubs. Blondie's hands and arms were now covered in blue tattoos with such words as 'Property of Butter'. Laughing, she lifted her skirt to reveal an even cruder sentence on her thigh. She admitted with pleasure that he was like a master and argued that perhaps she had always been looking for someone to protect and boss her.

My carefully-thought-out five-point plan – to enable Blondie to cope with her past and speak to Wally about his – faded into the background. Blondie's thoughts were now concentrated on Butter and she saw me just as a means of controlling the children and possibly finding baby-sitters.

I began to concentrate on spending time with Wally and June. It was partly that I wanted to avoid Butter, partly a wish to alleviate their suffering. June was now an active four-year-old. I would sit with her as she built up her bricks. Sometimes we would colour pictures together. When possible, I gave Wally his favourite drive in the mini-van.

On Wally's ninth birthday, I gave him a toy mini-van. He was delighted. Blondie provided a plastic football. He had no other presents. We strolled to the shop, with Wally all smiles as he ran the car along the tops of walls. His features, sharp and small, topped by straight brown hair, were not similar to Blondie's. I wondered if he resembled his dad, that Scotsman about whom he knew nothing. In the shop, Red Moore greeted us cheerily. Fortunately, Wally had not repeated his shoplifting. His wallpaper-picking had also ceased. Considering the changes he'd endured and the suicide attempt he'd witnessed, I reckoned he was doing remarkably well.

Blondie and Butter did not share my assessment. She complained that Wally followed her around the house, got under her feet. Eventually, she would explode and clip him around the ear. Then she complained that he was stealing money from her purse. When I argued that he was trying to win her attention, Blondie told me not to start the college-boy clap-trap again.

Wally also received harder wallops from Butter. To be fair, Butter sometimes romped around with him and had mock boxing-matches. But when he was in a black mood or had had too much booze, the six-foot man would lash out at the child. Wally was scared of his mum's lover. I saw it in his eyes. I heard it when Wally would pleadingly ask, 'Bob, when will he go?' I wanted to shield him, yet felt powerless to act.

Wally's fear was a fore-runner of Blondie's. Within a few months, her elation was replaced by despair. It was at this juncture that she made the Friday phonecall, 'Bob, you've got to help me.' We met furtively in the car, like two secret lovers. Tearfully she explained that the mastery had become slavery. Most, if not all, of the social security income had to be handed over to finance Butter Martin's pub activities. Consequently, bills went unpaid.

Blondie might have accepted this – she was accustomed to the financial tightrope – if Butter's love had remained undiminished. Now he grumbled about her slovenly house-work and failure to discipline the children. He complained that her leech-like attentions restricted him from talking to other women. When drunk, he smashed the furniture. He never sought employment, never lifted a finger in the home. To top it all, the Nutter had given her several blows and punches.

After she finished talking, I tried to reason.

'Blondie, you must tell him to go, or you and the kids will get smashed. The house is in your name. Let me tell him. If he won't leave I can fetch the police.'

'No, Bob. Promise you won't do that.' Her eyes were wide with terror. 'He said if I chucked him out he'd slash my face so that no other man would ever touch me. I must get back before he misses me. Please keep calling.'

My priggish satisfaction that Butter had turned out as I anticipated, was soon dispelled by my inability to help. I phoned Roger Driscoll at the Social Services Department. He explained that no action to remove the children to a place of safety could be taken without concrete evidence that Butter was harming them – and Blondie would not give evidence. He urged me to keep a close eye on developments.

Keep a close eye. More likely I'd get my eyes closed. I forced myself to call. Butter resented my 'interference', yet was prepared to admit I had some uses. I negotiated a repayment scheme just in time to prevent the Water Board cutting off supplies. He conceded that I amused the children. Sometimes we did talk together. He would spin yarns about how he fooled psychiatrists and social workers in prison in order to obtain the cushy jobs. He used the psychological jargon, creating the impression that he could also run rings around me. In turn, I stressed my concern for the children and conveyed the thinly-veiled threat that the local authority or police might have to intervene.

'Come upstairs,' shouted Blondie as I knocked one afternoon. There was rivalry between Butter and myself, and he was about to demonstrate his superior hold over Blondie. They were in bed together – naked. He began to fondle his woman while she laughed. Then he began to twist her breast until she gasped in pain.

'Don't worry,' grinned Butter. 'She loves me hurting her, don't you?' Blondie nodded, too scared to say no.

I was saved by hearing June cry. Ignoring Butter and asking Blondie's permission, I picked her up and went into the street where we found Wally. We went for a ride. Wally and June urged me to keep driving.

'Drive 100 miles, Bob,' Wally requested. 'Let's stay away until Butter goes.'

I could not desert them. I had to do something. Yet I was forced to admit to myself that I was only provoking Butter. I could see no way out of the mess. Butter was on to a good thing – easy money, good food, a woman he controlled. Blondie was too terrified to rebel. I could not imagine how it would end.

The end came suddenly. Another phonecall. This time from a neighbour at 11 p.m. She shrilly informed me that Butter was murdering Blondie and that Wally and June had run into her house. I got ready, my heart thumping in trepidation. Bet, white-faced, implored me to keep between Butter and a door. I had no idea what I would do. I slowed down and prayed.

'Lord, I need you so much. Please protect Blondie and

the children. And Lord protect me. You know I am scared; give me courage.'

A short prayer, a coward's prayer, but the prayer was answered. I felt calmer, more secure.

Turning into the path of Blondie's house, I looked up and saw Wally's terrified face pressed against a next-door neighbour's window. Absurdly, I gave him the thumbs-up sign. The front door opened to my push. Blondie was in the kitchen squatting in the corner. Her eyes were puffy, her cheeks marked.

'He's in the garden. He came back drunk. Wanted more money. He's had it all. He won't believe me. There's no food. He started to hit me and smash the furniture. I thought he'd kill us all. I managed to get Wally and June next door. He picked up the carving-knife as if to slash me. Then he wanted to puke up and went outside for some air.'

I decided what to do. 'Pack a bag, you and the kids are coming to my place.'

Blondie painfully climbed the stairs. She returned with a case. She had not packed for herself. She stood there, her blonde hair dishevelled, a trickle of blood running from her nose, her blouse torn at the shoulder. To my amazement, she sighed.

'Take the kids, Bob. I am not fit to have them. I will stay with him. I want him.'

Before I had time to answer, the back door flew open and Butter lurched in. There was no sign of the knife. He held a beer bottle in one hand. Fighting to control my feelings, I got to my feet.

'Blondie and the kids are coming with me. It's not safe here.'

I braced myself for a physical assault. I realized that I had forgotten Bet's advice, that Butter stood between me and the door. Perhaps he was too drunk or too sick to fight. He dropped into a chair and cradled his head in his arms on the kitchen table.

'Take them,' he slurred. 'I don't want them.'

Blondie moved towards him, her arms outstretched as though to cuddle him. He pushed her away.

'And take that cow. Useless in bed, useless in the home. Get her out.'

The words were as hurtful as a physical blow. Blondie's shoulders sagged. She bit her lips and her tongue tasted the blood on her face. She needed no further persuasion from me. Collecting Wally and June, we left. It was past midnight. Leaving the children with Bet, I drove to the hospital where she was X-rayed and detained.

The next morning I visited the Social Services Department. As a temporary measure, Roger agreed that the children should again go to Mrs Barnes. Later, as we were packing to go to the foster mum's again, I noticed that Wally had left his toy mini-van on the bookshelf. When I pointed it out to him, he replied, 'I know, I want to leave it here with you.'

Although the major traumas concerning Webster, Flo, Lorna, Phil and Blondie had been jammed into one week, the arguments, the funerals, the sortings out, the weepings, continued for a month. I had experienced previous setbacks but never anything so intense, so devastating as that month.

The last Saturday morning of the month, I lay gloomily in bed. Bet was already up, preparing breakfast. I should have been doing that. I felt too down, too emotionally and physically drained to move. Looking up, I stared at the gaping hole in the ceiling where Bet had fallen. Below stood the buckets still ready to catch the drips. The whole place was a mess. The Project was a mess.

Webster's face came to my mind. I still found it hard to stomach that he could have been so mean. The boy who had called me dad and who had hugged my wife had chosen the moment when Bet was in hospital and I was visiting her to creep into our home and steal the Project's money.

Flo's pretty, distressed, features were there, too. If I'd kept in touch over the last few months, I could have averted their financial crisis. Now her bloke had gone and she was as bereft, isolated and poverty-stricken as when I first met her.

And Lorna. I could not rid myself of the picture of the

mourning Lorna asking me, 'Why, why did my baby die?' How could I help her? I couldn't bring him back.

The father of another dead baby remained in a Midland jail. Phil had lost his loved ones and was near to losing his senses.

Not least, there was Blondie. Blondie with the battered face. Wally with the frightened face pressed against the window. June, who knew no face as that of her father.

The Project's three years were up. I almost hoped the money would not be renewed. Bet and I could move away. I'd retrain as a teacher. A 9–4 job with evenings and weekends to ourselves. A cosy home, a door that could be closed on the world outside.

'Bob, are you awake? That's the third time.'

I was aroused from my melancholy brooding by Bet's voice. Coffee was ready. Clambering into trousers and sweater, I went down to find Helen Shaw sitting with Bet.

'Hello, lazybones,' she greeted me. 'Listen, I've been talking to Dylan and Doreen and I don't think we're praying enough. I want you to give me a list of people who are in trouble or need. We'll all pray for them. Prayer has helped me so much, I ought to pray more for others.'

'That's a great idea, Helen,' I replied. 'I was upstairs worrying about my failures, forgetting that God is waiting to listen.'

Bet and Helen started to chat about young Francis, who had been in Bet's class at school. Helen's words had cheered me. To think I had once doubted if she would continue in the Christian way. The sheep had become the shepherd.

Rising to pour another coffee, I focussed on a grinning face looking down at me. Ted Williams was cleaning the windows. I waved him in and he joined us round the table. He asked for news about the Project being able to continue. The ever-smiling Ted became serious.

'Well, if you don't get the money, I hope you and Bet find some way of staying on. I tell you one thing, the streets are quieter now. The club and the sport give the kids something to do. You fit in here, so don't think you're going to leave. Now back to the cleaning.'

Ted was a hard worker. He operated all day Saturdays to ensure a reasonable income. He laughed and went. He left me with a glow. He was that kind of person. On his way out, Ted was met by Troy Peters banging on the door.

' 'Lo, Troy. What do you want?'

My usual greeting was 'come in'. Troy was taken aback at being asked why he had come. He wrinkled his face. His skin-head hair-cut above a thin body gave him the appearance of a lollipop.

'Dunno,' he answered. 'You've been so busy. Haven't seen you much. I missed you. Thought I'd come and see you.'

I laughed.

'Come on in, old son. Grab some toast.'

A few minutes later, Troy and I strolled up to the shop to collect the paper. Mrs Daphne Peters and Ken Standen were outside.

'Oh, there you are, Troy. I thought I told you to get some teabags. Don't matter. I was on my way to see Bob.' Daphne turned to me. 'Give me a kiss, Bob. We've got engaged.' She flashed a ring before my eyes as I planted a large kiss on her ample cheek and shook Ken's hand.

'Yes, my divorce is through. Ken proposed to me at bingo last week. So romantic.'

'And we want you to be best man,' Ken butted in. 'You've been a good friend to Daphne. You've stuck with Phil when we couldn't stand him. You'll do it, won't you?'

'Of course, I will. Proud to. I'll even give you some advice on married life.'

Daphne let out her trumpet-like laugh.

'There's not much you can teach us.'

I walked back with Troy. The people of Edgely might sometimes make me want to give up, but they also had the knack of lifting me up and making me want to survive.

10
Tipping the Scales

The offices of the Christian Community Council were located in a Victorian building in the West End of London. I was perched on a hard bench in the waiting-room. The room consisted mainly of polished wood, bookcases and oil paintings. I idly calculated that if the books and paintings were sold the proceeds could finance a score of community projects.

I was awaiting the CCC's decision whether the funding of the Edgely Project would be continued. Accompanied by Charlie Wantage, I had been questioned by the committee for nearly an hour. Floundering under a battery of rather remote questions, I was rescued by a very elderly lady with silver hair and a wrinkled face, introduced as Dame Edith Littlejohn. Here was someone who really understood what I was trying to say and posed the kind of questions which set me talking. I was able to explain my wish to be close to the residents, to be a friend not a superior, to participate as a member of the community and yet, at the same time, be available for help when required.

After grilling me, the committee turned to the written evidence. Charlie had submitted an assessment of my work. I had also written a report which had been duplicated and submitted beforehand. Charlie had told me that our town's police inspector had mailed in a statement which disapproved of my practice of refusing to report known juvenile offences. On the other hand, he praised my efforts to involve the local policeman in the youth club. Mr Senior on behalf of the magistrates, and Mr Black on behalf of the teachers, had also written letters in my favour. Most heart-warming of all, residents from Edgely had themselves organized a petition arguing for the continuation of the Project and even offering to raise money. Now that I realized the extent of local backing, I dearly wanted to stay on.

Nationally, the year had been marked by rising unemployment and some social unrest. One consequence was that the government had awarded the CCC a grant for 'use in promoting self-help to identify and solve problems in areas of social need'. So the committee had money. The issue, as Charlie put it to me, was whether they would opt to initiate new projects – always an attractive proposal – or whether they would be prepared to continue some existing ones. At that very moment, Charlie was with the committee trying to persuade them to back the latter course.

I had already been to the loo three times. My stomach kept churning over. To occupy my mind, I began reading again the report I'd submitted. It told of the clubs and activities which had been established. With names disguised, it also gave an account of the individuals I had tried to help.

Flicking over the pages, I came across my account of Webster Summerfield. The words reminded me of our earlier meetings, of his stormy personality, his need for a father figure, his continuous nicking. I smiled as I recalled the close relationships he had formed with Bet and myself. Then, just as he seemed to be solving his problems, came the shattering blow of his theft from our home.

The theft placed me in a difficult position. Mr Plumb spoke for the section of the community which considered he should be heavily punished. Refusing to involve the police, I pointed out that he had returned the money. On the other hand, the crime could not be overlooked.

After consultation with Bet and Dylan, we agreed that Webster should be banned from coming into our home for a month. The ban made him a lonely person, for he was already being cold-shouldered by the rest of the estate. He walked in fear of Legs Lancing who was threatening to beat him up. Shunned at the club, out of work, disgraced at home, he was in need of friendship. Yet when he knocked at our door each week to return a pound of the missing fiver, I could not invite him in. Our conversation was stilted and forced. Barriers of disappointment and hurt stood between us.

My fear was that Webster would revert to a life of crime. Instead, two factors began to tell in his favour. First, he obtained a job as a plumber's mate, where his ability to chat-up the customers proved useful to his employer. Once again he had money in his pocket and the prospect of a career. Second, he started going steady with Alison Smart, a slim brunette who worked as a typist in the plumber's office. Living in Blackway, she took no notice of Webster's general unpopularity and was charmed by his lively manner and sense of humour. She possessed a determined spirit and, after Webster told her about his delinquent exploits, exerted pressure on him to go straight. They came together just at the time when he most needed affection and someone with whom to spend his spare time. Thus, unexpectedly his life took a more stable turn.

The emotional rift between Webster and myself was finally patched up with the assistance of our bathroom taps. In attempting to replace a washer, I made my usual botch-up and couldn't replace the nut. Feeling foolish, I phoned a plumber.

'All right, sir, I'll send the lad round,' he replied in a tone which implied that a small boy could capably do the job.

The lad proved to be a grinning Webster. Fixing the tap in about thirty seconds, he tried to talk me into having a shower installed. Declining, I made some coffee instead.

'Cor, can I drink this coffee? Is my suspension up now?' he asked with a laugh.

'It is, I'm glad to say. Welcome back to the Laken home. It hasn't been the same without you.'

He continued chatting, holding forth with equal enthusiasm about his love for Alison and burst pipes. Changing the subject, he said seriously:

'I still don't know why I stole that money. I felt in the grip of evil. I felt terrible afterwards, it's been like a ton of lead pipes on my mind. I've ruined our friendship. I want to do something to make up for it.'

I put my hand on his shoulder.

'Thanks, Webster. I reckon you've suffered enough. As far as I'm concerned the slate is wiped clean. Just keep out of trouble from now on.'

He rose to move on to his next job. Seeing him dressed in workman's overalls and carrying a tool bag, I realized that his boyish days were over. He refused any payment for the job. At the door, he turned.

'Once you took me to Ebenezer and Ted was talking about a lost boy who returned home and his father forgave him all the things he did wrong. I understand that story now.'

He closed the door and I watched through the window as he revved up his motor bike with a roar that made the passing Mrs Battle jump in the air with shock. With a blast on the horn, he sped away.

In the waiting-room, I went on to the next page of the report. It concerned the Scott family. Flo had considered her life finished when Ritchie walked out during that dreadful week. In debt, fearful of the cruelty man, possibly pregnant and deserted by her bloke, Flo had turned to me again. A phone-call to the NSPCC reassured the Inspector that Flo was not a cruel mother. An equally sympathetic official at the Electricity Board listened while I explained Flo's troubles. It was agreed that she repay the debts over a year and the threat of cutting off her supply was withdrawn. Next, I drove her to the doctor's to see if she was pregnant. Nothing could be done about Ritchie, as his whereabouts were unknown.

Ritchie was missing for nearly a month. The crisis brought out the best in Fiona and Mac. Fiona contributed most of her wage-packet towards household expenses. In the evenings, she was prepared to help with the housework. The hostility and resentment which had formerly come between daughter and mother was over. Mac, too, responded positively. He curbed his loud mouth and even volunteered to look after Ishbael.

One evening, as the family sat talking, Mac asked his mum if Ritchie's departure was like that of his real dad, all those years before. For the first time, Flo was able to speak to them about her soldier husband, about the romance of being

176

a teenage bride, about the difficulties of being a teenage mother. She explained that she had hidden the truth about their dad for fear that Mac and Fiona would despise her past failures and would want to return to their father. The very expression of her worry drew forth denials from the children. As Mac put it:

'Mum, you've fallen out with neighbours, with Joe, with Ritchie, but never once have you stopped looking after us. We couldn't leave you.'

Flo had reared the children as a tightly-bound, insular, unit. Now, as they understood more about her struggles and anxieties, they were ready to respond as a family who would stand together. Later, recounting these incidents to me, Flo said that despite all the agony surrounding Ritchie's leaving, she would not have missed for anything those moments with her children.

Then Ritchie phoned me. Far from being with another woman, he was staying with an uncle in a nearby town.

'Haven't got long, I'm in a callbox. I was mad to walk out on Flo. Can't stand it any longer. Please get her to ring me now.'

Remembering to take his number, I dashed to get Flo. Her eyes lit up and, within a few moments, she was speaking to her beloved. Three hours later, he was back home. The reunion was like a scene from a TV soap opera. Two bodies propelled themselves into each other's arms. Tears were shed, kisses exchanged, apologies given and life-long promises made, all in the space of two minutes. The month apart seemed to have strengthened their love. Once again, they were to be seen hand-in-hand as they walked along Edgely's muddy and lamp-posted streets.

Soon after, Flo and Ritchie invited me to participate in a long and serious discussion. They had decided to marry, once legally free. Flo's only regret was that she was not pregnant after all. She added that they would keep on trying. From what I could guess, they would enjoy the trying very much. But they had really invited me in to talk finances. Together we made a weekly budget of the money they had to put aside for vital bills. They agreed that Ritchie would go to the pub just once a week until he obtained employment.

Not long after, Ritchie found a job with a band of men who travelled the affluent south coast doing gardening jobs. His departure sent alarm bells ringing in my mind, for it seemed a repetition of Flo's history with Joe. I need not have worried. Ritchie returned home every weekend and enjoyed yet more embraces from the pining Flo. Further, he handed over most of his earnings. No doubt the gardening pickings would cease in the winter but, for the first time, the family had a generous income.

I continued to call occasionally. If Ritchie was away, Flo would merely open the window and speak across the sill. Obviously, she felt she could now cope without my assistance. At first, I was a little taken aback. On reflection, I felt pleased that the family was sufficiently independent to make do without a social worker.

Smiling, I closed the page on the Scotts. The smile vanished as I turned to the next family in the report – the Thomases. The pain of Clint's death and Lorna's grief still lingered in my mind. I read quickly, as though to avoid my record of those dark days, and sped on to the words I had penned as a conclusion.

Soon after the funeral, Stirling Drift returned from Newcastle. Although he had never secured work there, he had found some money, for he drove a new Cortina. No doubt, Lorna's emotions were stirred by his return. Probably she had a fantasy about a new, reliable, faithful, hardworking Mr Drift, who would love and care for her and Elvis.

No such Mr Drift existed. He visited his old love just once. Not mentioning the death of Clint, he took hardly any notice of Elvis. Instead, he chose to inform Lorna that he had moved in with a girl in Blackway. Big-hearted as ever, he added that he was still 'willing to have a bit on the side' with Lorna.

Her reply was to the effect that she would rather go with the hunchbuck of Notre Dame. She could have taken the yo-yo playing with her emotions. She would not accept his

178

callous approach to the babies she loved. The spell was broken.

The dashing of her hopes about Stirling, following so fast on the death of her son, led to depression. Ron Keen, worried that Lorna's apathy was affecting her attitude towards Elvis, dropped in to talk to me.

'There's no point in pumping anti-depressant pills into her,' he confided. 'She needs something that will give her purpose in life, something to boost her confidence. At present, she is overwhelmned by her failure to look after Clint and her failure with this guy Drift. People who help in your Project seem to lift themselves up. Could you do something for her?'

I shook my head.

'At this stage, I can't see Lorna wanting to help in the junior club. But I've got another idea. Red Moore was talking of taking on another part-timer at the shop. That would bring her into contact with other people and show her that she can do a job.'

Ron agreed. Red agreed. Lorna was dubious. She gloomily pointed out that she had missed most of her last two years at school and had never held any kind of job. Nonetheless, with encouragement from her mum, brother and myself, she decided to have a go.

Becky had given up her bookshop post, so she now cared for the baby while Lorna worked afternoons. She already knew Toni at the shop and soon began enjoying the banter and gossip that went on there. Her quickness and efficiency on the till soon earned the approval of Red. Her wages did much to replace those lost by Becky. More important, as Lorna took an interest in, and was appreciated by, customers and staff, her depression began to recede.

While Lorna was at her lowest ebb, Roly Williams, Doreen Willis and Bet had joined with Mrs Plumb and Toni Hale to make sure that she was never short of company. The friendships formed were such that, once Lorna started work, they decided to meet together once a week in our house. During the school holidays, they met on Wednesday mornings, with the children in one room as a kind of impromptu playgroup and the mothers in a nearby room. Once term restarted, Bet could no longer attend but the others determined not only to continue but also to invite others to their women's group.

The support of family and friends enabled Lorna to survive. Her love and care for Elvis was rekindled. She even began to have a few dates with the driver of the bakery van which delivered daily to the shop. The questions and scars left by death and rejection still remained and sometimes reduced her to tears. Nonetheless, most of the time she appeared to be coping with her child, her circumstances and her emotions.

Reading on, I came to my remarks about Phil Peters. Following his attack on Lucy, he came close to a mental and physical breakdown. The chaplain, Richard Menzies, subsequently told me that he had nearly been moved to a psychiatric hospital. To Richard must go much of the credit for the fact that the breakdown was averted. He patiently accepted Phil's anger, insults and grief. Gradually, the strange mixture of sadness and madness began to lift.

The young prisoner found solace in two directions. He began an art class. Later he told me that he chose art because the teacher was one of the few good-looking women to enter the prison. But he did actually possess a talent for painting, a talent which had never been spotted let alone developed at school. At first, he drew picture after picture of baby Greta. Then savage paintings of Lucy and her lover. Finally, peaceful memories of the Lake District.

In addition, Phil sought strength in his Christian faith. He liked to spend time alone in the chapel and held long discussions with Richard about the meaning of the tragedies that had blighted his life.

I visited once a month. On the second occasion, Daphne Peters accompanied me. In the course of a tearful reunion, the son expressed regret that he had ended up in prison, the mother wept over his shattered life. Daphne promised Phil that she would now visit regularly.

During this visit, Phil asked me to bring Drew Sprite.

180

'Bring him here, Bob,' he urged. 'Let him see what a wreck I am. I'll tell him about the beatings up, the strong men who cry, the old lags who will die in prison. One visit will be enough to warn him what will happen if he follows me.'

Years of imprisonment still lay ahead. The years might crush him, force him into more violence, break his sanity. Or his new beliefs and outlets might enable him to survive. I did not know. I could only hope – and pray.

The last account in my report concerned Blondie Blake and her children. As the words reminded me of their ups and downs, my reactions ranged from amusement, to despair, to hope. Following the beating-up of Blondie, the hospital authorities informed the police of her injuries. The slighted Blondie now decided that her best protection was to get Butter put away. She not only described his assault on herself but also grassed on his criminal activities. Butter was arrested, charged, held on remand and seemed certain to receive a long sentence.

Discharging herself from the hospital, Blondie returned home. To my surprise, she made no effort to contact the children or me. When I called, her house was locked and unlived in. A tip from Dickie Driver led me to a decaying, Victorian building in the town centre. It was occupied by squatters who initially refused to supply any information. Fortunately, a thin youth with a black beard turned out to be a drop-out from a social work training course. As we conversed, he expressed approval of the kind of work I was doing, which he contrasted with the 'management-dominated hierarchies in local authority departments'. Eventually, he revealed that Blondie, after a couple of nights at the squat had shacked up with a biker and was last seen perched on the back of his machine as they sped off to Cornwall.

The same evening Blondie phoned me from a callbox.

'It's me, Blondie. Don't try to find me. I had to get away. Need time to think. I'll go mad if I don't have some peace. Look after the kids.'

She put down the receiver before I could complete a

sentence. The next morning, I reported the events to Roger Driscoll at the Social Services Department. He rapidly made some decisions. Despite my opposition, he argued that Mrs Barnes was too old to care for Wally and June on a long-term basis. The children were to be received into the care of the local authority and placed in an Assessment Centre, where plans for their future could be carefully worked out. Further, he declared that Blondie's promiscuity and her abandonment of the children constituted sufficient grounds for the council to remove her parental rights.

Roger granted me one favour. He allowed me to break the news to Wally and June. As best I could, I described to them why mum had gone away. Hardly able to hold back my tears, I explained why they would have to leave Mrs Barnes. June, as usual, wet her pants. Wally's face took on that old, defiant, aggressive, look.

'Bob, you won't leave me, will you?'

'Wally, I promise I'll see you every week for as long as you want.'

A month went by while two vacancies were awaited at the Assessment Centre. Yet they never went there. Perhaps they should have done but the council had never before come up against Blondie Blake. One lunchtime, she marched through the open back door into our house.

'I'm back,' she bawled. Sitting on the table, she crossed one leg over the other, deliberately revealing her sun-tanned thighs. She was dressed in blue denim. I had never seen her looking so well. Her blonde hair contrasted with her bronzed skin. Her eyes shone with health. Those white teeth flashed as she smiled at me.

'Blondie, where have you been?' I exploded and proceeded to tell her that she was about to lose the kids along with her rights as a mother. Blondie stood up. Unusually composed and calm, she replied:

'We'll see about that. Let's call on this Mr Driscoll.'

An hour later, Blondie and I sat in a small cubicle known as an interviewing-room. Roger entered and came straight to the point, informing Blondie that her abandonment of the children left the Social Services Department no choice but to take them into care. Steps were being taken to assume complete powers over them on the grounds that her changing of partners made her unfit to be a mother. Blondie casually flicked a speck of dust from her skirt and made a speech with the confidence and air of a female lawyer in an American TV serial.

'Mr Driscoll, you've got your facts all wrong. You know I suffered a severe beating-up and had to enter hospital and then go on holiday to recover. I left the children in the safe hands of Bob Laken. I did not abandon them. Now, as to my changing partners – you make it sound like a barn dance – and you're implying that I am some kind of a tart. As a respectable married woman, I resent that and my husband might well give you a present of a bunch of fives in the mouth.'

'Married? Husband?' I gasped.

With a flourish, Blondie opened her bag and threw a marriage certificate on the table. In a Cornish registry office, she had married the biker, Mr William Tanner.

'Now, I'm going to collect my kids. *My* kids, Mr Social Worker. And if you try to stop me, I'll go straight to the newspapers. Come on, Bob.'

Roger was dumb. He wiped and re-wiped his spectacles. He ran his hand through his few remaining hairs. I looked at him, shrugged my shoulders, and meekly followed the amazing Blondie Tanner.

Wally and June were overjoyed to see Blondie and accepted, almost as routine, the propect of meeting a new dad. The following weeks were happy ones. Bill Tanner was an unusual man. In his thirties, he was a cross between a biker and a hippie. His long hair and unkempt beard hid a kindly nature and quick sense of humour. He related well to the children, who adored rides on his powerful motor bike. I felt at ease in his presence and the three of us would converse for hours.

Blondie was now keen to trace her half-sister, Nora. She argued again that her own insecurity and restlessness sprang from her lack of roots, the absence of relatives. Through Miss Roberts, I had established the name of the village where

Nora had settled with her dad. Despite the passing years, I was confident that a small community would have knowledge of her whereabouts. As we planned to visit the village, I again challenged Blondie to talk to Wally about his dad. Bill supported me by pointing out that Wally too was subject to the anxieties of not knowing the truth about his background. Blondie agreed to do so at a convenient moment.

Blondie's current stability did not deceive me. Despite the happiness of the honeymoon period, I could see the seeds of future troubles. Bill was a drifter who worshipped his motor bike. His refusal to work – or as he put it, his 'rejection of the capitalist work ethic' – would eventually annoy Blondie, who wanted more money to run the home. In time, I guessed he would leave. Blondie's high period would be replaced by a low one.

Perhaps Roger Driscoll was right when he argued that Wally and June's long-term well-being would be best served by permanent removal from their mother. Yet I knew that mother and children loved and wanted each other. I hoped that Blondie was learning from experience and from insights into her past so that she would become more settled, more reliable. If possible, I wanted to be on hand to help her.

Would I be on hand to help Blondie and other Edgely residents? I was about to learn. A woman with shoulder-length grey hair and an ankle-length grey skirt politely requested me to step back into the committee room. Sitting in a hard-backed chair, I scanned the solemn faces before me. Then Dame Edith winked at me and I knew all was well. The bishop-chairman pronounced sentence like a judge.

'Normally, Mr Laken, the CCC does not renew grants. We view ourselves as pump primers, as sparks which light fires whose flames must be rekindled by others, as seed sowers whose young plants must be nurtured by different farmers.' He paused to give effect to his sermon-like exposition.

'However, the government in its wisdom has awarded us grants specifically for use in areas of need where local people can be encourged to help. Your project fits this brief. Thus your salary will be continued for a further three years – with an addition for inflation. Further, after reading your report, we deem it appropriate that you have a fellow worker from the neighbourhood. At the suggestion of the vicar of St Matthew's, we propose to ask Mr Dylan Willis to join you, if you so wish.'

I left in a daze. On the train back, Charlie disclosed that Dame Edith had taken a liking to my ideas and had pleaded my case. Apparently she was a powerful voice in the social work world and Charlie recommended that I invite her down to see the project. It was Dame Edith, too, who recommended that a person born and bred in the area be appointed alongside me. Charlie had immediately thought of Dylan.

Back home, I broke the news to a delighted Bet and we both hurried round to the Willis's, even though it was gone ten o'clock. When I broached the possibility of Dylan joining the project, he and Doreen looked at each other and fell silent. Puzzled, I asked if I had upset them.

'No, Bob, just the opposite,' Dylan replied. 'Over the last few weeks I've been saying to Doreen that I'd love a job like yours. It seemed impossible. I've no qualifications. We've prayed about it. And now you walk through the door with this offer. We're just overcome. When do I start?'

With no games or clubs organized, Sunday was usually an easygoing casual day. Youngsters might drift in for a chat, parents for a coffee. Those so inclined would accompany Bet and myself to Ebenezer in the evening.

The Sunday following the CCC meeting, I was still in an elated mood. The news spread around the estate and various residents dropped in to express their pleasure. Helen Shaw, on her way to the morning service at St Matthew's ran in and gave me an unexpected hug.

'I'll be singing thanks to God this morning,' she cried.

Ruby Curtis and Fangs Battle bounced in to make plans for more clubs, a junior football team and a girl's hockey match. They both declared that they wanted to be helpers in the new activities.

'We might even be like Dylan one day,' exclaimed the excited Fangs.

Later, Webster arrived with Alison. Bet had not yet met his girl-friend and Webster was anxious to introduce them. She listened shyly while Webster recounted his adventures and friendship with us. I felt like a Victorian father whose son was presenting his beloved for paternal approval.

After tea, Bet and I drove the short distance to Ebenezer. Ted Williams, delighted that we were staying on, wore an even wider smile than usual. Every other Sunday, he chose his favourite hymn, 'Oh for a thousand tongues to sing my great Redeemer's praise' and this week he roared away as though they were already his. In his short talk, Ted described how Jesus Christ delighted to mix with the ordinary folk, with the poor, the rejected – with, as he put it, 'the riff-raff like me'. His words struck a note in my heart. In the past I had listened to learned sermons preached by bishops, archbishops, professors and doctors of theology. Yet none of them had so graphically portrayed the meaning of Christianity as this window cleaner. For some reason, I felt overwhelmingly thankful that I had come to Edgely.

We rose to sing the last hymn. As I stood at the back, my eyes scanned the congregation. Roly Williams and her daughters sang so lustily that I thought Miss Bird would be blown off the organ. Dylan, Doreen and Rebecca Willis were in their accustomed places at the front. Elderly Mr Blenknsop's bald head was so shiny that the electric light beams bounced off at an angle. Dear old Mrs Barnes, who had done so much for Blondie's children, held the hymn-book close to her failing eyes. Drew Sprite, as ever, was infuriating others by poking them and trying to move the pew when they sat down.

At the back with me were Jardine Peters, Don Plumb, Mac Scott and Jules Thomas. Still feeling a bit self-conscious about attending chapel they declined to sing the hymns and kept their eyes open during prayers. But they continued to come. As I looked around, I felt a closeness to them all. They were my neighbours and friends. Sometimes I had helped them and sometimes they had enriched my life.

Jardine waited to speak to me at the chapel door. I expected him to say something about the extension of the grant. Instead, he asked, 'Bob, tell me, how do I become a Christian?'

His question both unnerved and excited me. Unnerved because I felt inadequate to provide a full answer. Excited because he was asking the most important question of all. We sat on the stone wall and talked. I left him with a copy of the New Testament and a promise to talk again when he had read more about Jesus Christ.

Bet shared in my happiness. She put her arm around me and kissed me lightly on the cheek as I directed the mini-van back to the house.

'You should see your face,' she laughed. 'You're like the cat with the cream. Why, there's Wally outside.'

The van's headlights had caught Wally, leaning against our door. For a moment, I thought another disaster had struck. Instead, he thrust a note from Blondie, asking for the loan of a pound, into my hand. I handed the money to him.

'Hey, Wally,' I called, as he prepared to run home. 'Your mini-van is still in the bedroom. Do you want to take it?'

His thin features broke into a grin.

'No. I know it's there for when I need it. Like you. I know you're always here if I need you.'

Clutching the pound note, he raced away into the darkness.

Sorry to Bother You Doctor
Andrew Hamilton

'Sorry to bother you doctor, but . . .' Andrew Hamilton hears that phrase some twenty times a day in his surgery. And drawing on his experience in general practice, he has brought together this highly entertaining collection of stories of the everyday trials and tribulations of his patients. With its warmth and humour Doctor Hamilton's book is better than a dose of medicine!

It's Me Again, Doctor
Andrew Hamilton

For convinced fans and new readers alike, Doctor
Hamilton tells us more fascinating stories from his years
in general practice. The time his barber collapsed in
agony half-way through cutting his hair . . . how a
grateful patient sprayed his car with dung . . . his
experience as medical officer at a wrestling-bout . . .
and many others. Now it's your turn for a fresh injection
of warmth, wisdom and wit. Next one for the doctor,
please . . .